DEMOLISHING NISARD

other works by Eric Chevillard in English translation

Palafox
The Crab Nebula
On the Ceiling

DEMOLISHING NISARD
ERIC CHEVILLARD

translated by Jordan Stump

Dalkey Archive Press
Champaign / Dublin / London

Library of Congress Cataloging-in-Publication Data

Chevillard, Éric.
[Démolir Nisard. English]
Demolishing Nisard / Eric Chevillard ; translated by Jordan Stump. -- 1st ed.
p. cm.
Originally published in French as Démolir Nisard.
ISBN 978-1-56478-633-3 (pbk. : alk. paper)
1. Nisard, D. (Désiré), 1806-1888--Fiction. I. Stump, Jordan, 1959- II. Title.
PQ2663.H432C4613 2011
843'.914--dc22
                    2011014809

Partially funded by a grant from the Illinois Arts Council, a state agency, and by the University
of Illinois at Urbana-Champaign

Ouvrage publié avec le concours du Ministère français chargé de la culture – Centre national
du livre

This work has been published, in part, thanks to the French Ministry of Culture – National
Book Center

www.dalkeyarchive.com

Cover: design and composition by Danielle Dutton, illustration by Nicholas Motte
Printed on permanent/durable acid-free paper and bound in the United States of America

According to Désiré Nisard, French literature fell into an irreversible decline with the death of Bossuet and the end of the seventeenth century, an opinion he expressed in 1835, so imagine how things must have gone downhill since, imagine the distaste he would surely have felt for *this* book, dating as it does from the early years of the twenty-first. And no, it will not be written in the style of the Latin classics so dear to his heart, but such a flaw would have been only the pretext seized upon by old two-face Nisard to justify his disdain: we're not that naïve. No great outlay of brainpower is required to surmise the true source of his scorn. After all, what is the primary target of the present broadside? Désiré Nisard himself, flushed with shame. And rightly so, for the aim of these pages' author is clear, and boldly proclaimed from the start: he means to destroy Désiré Nisard, and then his work will be done. That's a solemn vow. I'm going to sic my dogs on him, loose my falcons, lay waste to his orchards, brutalize his family, do you hear? I'm going to demolish Désiré Nisard.

Strange project, Métilde tells me, going on to ask who this Désiré Nisard might be, as if that creature deserved anyone's interest. And like a shot comes my reply: Désiré Nisard? Virtually no one knows who he is, and in any case who gives a damn?

What kind of a name is Nisard? Désiré Nisard? Can people really be called Désiré Nisard? Jean-Marie-Napoléon-Désiré Nisard? Listen, Métilde, I repeat: Jean-Marie-Napoléon-Désiré Nisard. Who could possibly bear such a name? I believe that'll give you a sense of the man. Who could possibly bear such a name, save, precisely, and as if by chance, Jean-Marie-Napoléon-Désiré Nisard? Needless to say, there's more to that sordid buffoon than we can learn from his name. But already we might, in all serenity, observe that Désiré Nisard is far from the most illustrious of all Napoléons.

Neither is it forbidden to turn to Pierre Larousse's *Great Universal Dictionary of the Nineteenth Century* and consult the appropriate entry, an on-the-spot report, written while the old fart was still animate, a document all the more precious in that it issues from one who witnessed firsthand the doings of this **NISARD** (*Jean-Marie-Napoléon-Désiré*), *French critic, born in Châtillon-sur-Seine*

(Côte d'Or) in 1806. After completing his studies at the Collège Sainte-Barbe, Monsieur Nisard embarked on a journalistic career, whereby he would prove that a man can go places in journalism, provided he gets out of it—an axiom much in vogue under the July Monarchy. From his beginnings at the Journal des Débats *and* Le National, *he would rise to the ranks of Representative in the Chambre des Députés, head of the École Normale, and member of the Académie Française.* As we see, Larousse maintains an uncomfortable silence on the subject of Désiré's childhood, which is entirely to the good lexicographer's credit, and indeed we shall have many more occasions to admire the nobility of his soul and the kindliness of his heart, not to mention his commendable self-restraint, for the young Nisard was a wearisome brat, whiny, secretive, capricious, irresolute, fearful, forever smearing his shirtsleeves with the snot that flowed unquenchably from his ridiculous nose, a filthy habit he is said to have kept up until an advanced age, despite the many remonstrations doled out by his parents, whose other two sons, Charles and Auguste, nevertheless gave them every satisfaction. "*My father was an upstanding man, his integrity equal to all challenges, his every act rooted in virtue,*" Nisard would belatedly acknowledge, and his mother too was a very sweet lady, utterly without guile. The name she chose for her child tells us eloquently enough how eagerly his coming was awaited. In spite of which, somewhat adrift in the billows of infant apparel designed for a far more robust child, the sickly newborn continually soils his diapers and regurgitates his milk, devoting the remaining hours of his day to endless wailing. Such were the first months of an existence that

would in years to come eschew no mode of expression by which complaints might be voiced.

A vile little snitch, a talented pupil by virtue of his limited imagination and innate servility, further endowed with the phenomenal memory of the slow-witted, whose brains are close cousins to sponges and moss, Désiré makes a natural target for schoolboy bullies, but he gives as good as he gets, his fearless fist crushing every ladybug and ant that comes within reach. The head-louse, on the other hand, finds a warm welcome in his drab, stringy hair.

How can you possibly know all this? asks Métilde. Oh, nothing could be simpler. Read just two or three lines from the pen of that sinister spouter of pieties and all will be revealed: you'll understand at once where he came from—from what rotten egg, from what frustrated childhood he sprouted. But surely Métilde has better things to do than dispatch some librarian into a dusty back room to retrieve the four volumes of Nisard's *History of French Literature*, sealed shut by damp and a century of readerly neglect, better things to do than sacrifice a few precious hours of her youth, her fascinating beauty, to those pages. How it would pain me to see Métilde sunk waist-deep in that swamp! Métilde mired in the gray muck of those tomes, and Nisard slithering along the muddy bottom like a slimy reptile, coiling around her ankles, Nisard holed up in the cavity of his utterly empty life's work, that sad wad of wood-pulp, ever on the lookout for fresh, nubile prey after decades of bitter solitude precious little enlivened by the passing visit of some hurried academic in search of a reference for a footnote, Nisard sprawled in his own filth, suddenly lunging on catching sight of Métilde's rosy foot, his flabby lips suckering onto it, Nisard whose secret depravity I've long suspected, able to conceal it no longer, powerless to choke it back after so long an abstinence, throwing himself on her, slavering and spluttering, his eyes wild, his manner deranged.

I will not be held responsible for my actions if Nisard lays one hand on Métilde. We meet at dawn on the drear plain of Waterloo, Napoléon Nisard! And there you will learn what it means to die a thousand deaths, since apparently yours wasn't enough for you, rid this world though it did of your tiresome presence, I have nine hundred ninety-nine more to inflict on you, shall I count the ways? Some involve an unleashing of giant squids or rattlesnakes, others require only a little girl's sharpened fingernail or a pinch of ground glass. There's one I'm particularly fond of, a bit slow in coming, you'll see, where the executioner is a rat. If Nisard lays one hand on Métilde, I will collect his clay-coated ashes and shape them into a grimacing mask, its features contorted in horror, which I will then bake in a kiln—and thus will Désiré Nisard pass into posterity. And should his splintered coffin reveal some small pile of bones, I will stuff them with well-larded meat, to reawaken the interest of passing stray dogs. And the handful of teeth I might gather will soon be gnashing anew, grating horribly, I swear I'll find a way. Nisard, you foul brute, hands off my woman! Nisard,

I'll sink my teeth into you, cut you into tiny pieces, into dice, into shreds. You haven't felt the last of my rage.

"Firmly believing that literature must take its place as a discipline alongside the teachings of hearth and home, the principles of religion, the laws of the fatherland, I have studied our great writers less for their artistry than for their authority as judges of men's thoughts and deeds, less for their exceptionality than for the universally wise counsel they offer us, by which they participate in our lives, like beloved masters whose every word we obey," proclaims Désiré Nisard, for example. So it's a master he wants? I'll give him a master. I'll make him crawl. Fond of the whip, are you, Nisard? I suspected just some such turpitude. You're purring in my claws, aren't you? Your little cries are cries of pleasure. Very well, then: I must take up some more drastic weapon. There are, after all, blades that dispense only a very imperfect sort of ecstasy.

I wouldn't say no to a little help. Join me. Let's go after him together, a pack of us on his tail, ten or twenty strong. Come lend me a hand, at least two of you. You hold him down and I'll work him over. His belly will feel the wrath of my fist, his face will know the ire of my foot. I'll aim for his privates: that animal has reproduced all too prolifically as it is. High time we called a halt to that lineage, time we stanched the flow of that spunk, teeming with the morbid agents of Nisard's propagation like a tadpole-clogged mud puddle, gushing from him in gouts like a hemorrhage. Let's close that wound. Sew it up with iron wire. Weld it shut. Too many sons already have seen the light of day, now spread to the four corners of the globe. No hope of tracking them down and slaughtering them one by one, let's not kid ourselves. But what matter: we've got our hands on the mastermind of that crime against humanity. We've got our hands on the ringleader of that rank misdeed. We've got our hands on Désiré Nisard. He's a dead man. Let him harbor no hope of clemency. Saint Désiré will be stoned, flayed, and fed to the lions. And then once a year we will faithfully commemorate his martyrdom with orgiastic celebrations, my friends, with what unbridled revelries! Hold him tight, don't let him go. Oh, it feels so good to throw a punch sometimes. With every blow that lands, the wretch crumples a little more. Whence it is no longer entirely senseless to dream of a book without Nisard.

To which—like a private park, a sylvan glade, like the moon— we might retire, fleeing the clamor and commotion of stories, all those eternal stories, forever starting up anew, and the authority of all those judges of our thoughts and deeds, all swept away now, like the plains the day after the dinosaurs' demise, and there we would find a place of repose, a retreat, with no God either, nor any new face to contend with—or else, briefly, the smug face of some top-hatted passerby who would soon weary of bending down to retrieve his battered headgear from the dust, and would thus choose not to linger—and no mechanics of cause and effect to ensnare us in their workings, no gears beneath our cogged feet, no suspense to arouse our spurious interest in mysteries so hollow and in reality so devoid of interest that their resolution deflates us like a cheap confidence trick, like a promise unkept, like a woman of sand, it would still be a book of course, but one where nothing would happen as it does in other books, a book without Nisard, a book perhaps written solely for the purpose of staking out its territory and defending that turf against all the other books that would otherwise soon come crowding in, of preventing incursions by any book like every other book, with their efficient little systems, every stitch in place, the needlework starts up on the very first page, a thousand seamstresses at their task, a thousand worker ants, multiplying by many times the weariness of what's to follow, the eternal story lurching once more into action, death at work, a book in which the undesirable Nisard would find no air to breathe, and the teachings of hearth and home, of religion, of the laws of the fatherland, would wither and fade alongside him, a book in which all the innumerable things of this world would be swallowed up, in which everything would disappear.

A volume of blank pages wouldn't do it. It would want to be filled up, left to right and top to bottom, like a schoolboy's notebook—whereupon everything would once again be understood, justified—or else it would constitute a ceaseless temptation for writers. The moment they laid eyes on it, fingered its pages, they would feel their principal organs stirring inside them, like so many sons eager to be born: and with this their poetic souls would begin holding forth, their intellects gearing up, and above all their imaginations, their lively imaginations, frantically hunting around for memories to exploit. No, the book I have in mind, at least within the space it will clear for itself, means to escape their control, their mastery, their passion for meaning, their taste for detail, their life-like descriptions—just like looking out on the world through a pristine window, sometimes, wouldn't you say?—their gift for the narrative art. Oh no, this time we're not going to shuffle down that hallway, into that tunnel, this time we're not going to stick our heads, ankles, and wrists into those nooses. We won't let ourselves be snared in those traps, taken in by those tricks, not this time. We've played along all too indulgently. How docile we were! And always up for any new adventure. You will walk on two legs, it was ordained, for example—and everyone, or nearly, falls right into line! Just look around you, if you're not convinced. And we'll all move those two legs in the same way, and always for the purpose of heading off to some new destination. Our planet resounds with the footfalls of that forced march. Are our noses so thin from having been so long pinched and tugged forward between the thumbs and index fingers of our beloved masters, whose every word we obey? And did our knees grow so round from having so long rolled and rubbed against other knees in the great human tide that also knocks one skull against the next, like pebbles tumbling in the surf? The book without Nisard would be an opportunity for blessed solitude at long last.

Rigor and steadfastness are merely the frock coat and knee breeches of Désiré Nisard's ceremonial attire. In reality, no one is more flexible. The elasticity of his spine is an object of burning envy for every slithering snake and slug under the reign of Louis-Philippe. Once an ardent backer of this latter's rule, he later migrates into the Liberal camp; these about-faces would become the hallmark of a life lived in unwavering compliance with the dictates of an absolute ideal inextricably entwined with that loathsome courtier's private ambition and hunger for honors, and indeed under each successive regime, no matter its stripe, he would thrive: he must have had enough snake oil stored up to grease every weather vane in Paris. But do you suppose he did? Oh, no! All for him! Larousse's portrait of Nisard continues: *In the literary realm, he just as readily threw in his lot with the school of whimsy, publishing a risqué little novel,* A Milkmaid Succumbs *(1831, in-octavo), that would later cause the stern critic and Academician more than one sleepless night. No trace of* A Milkmaid Succumbs *remains: it is claimed that Monsieur Nisard spent a part of his life seeking out copies of that book and destroying them.* And here two contrary regrets simultaneously skewer our hearts.

For one thing, we regret the impossibility of reading *A Milkmaid Succumbs.* For all evidence suggests that Nisard did in fact succeed in wiping every last copy from the face of this earth. No mention of that title in the catalogs of the most prestigious libraries. I'll admit, I haven't exactly moved mountains to dig it up. There are beaches to be lounged on, pipes to be smoked, a thousand other things to do tomorrow before one might think of launching into an endless quest for that moldy fleece. But we would happily read it if it did fall into our hands, gladly skim Nisard's saucy tale, whose utter flatness we can nonetheless easily deduce—this flatness being its one innovation, seen against the heaving, curvaceous backdrop of conventional erotica—from the devastating ineptitude of his later writings. And perhaps then, I tell myself, once I've demolished Nisard, it will also put paid to the nightmare of obliteration that visits a man at the very height or in the very depths of his pleasures. To be sure, Désiré Nisard is a master of classical French prose, but he has to count out the measures and beats, a superficial technician, the uninspired interpreter of music composed by others: not even the finest drumhead will resonate when it's stretched over a tree stump.

The title of Nisard's ribaldry bespeaks clearly enough the poverty of his imagination: his very libido inspires in him only the most pitifully banal sort of fantasy. Is there then nowhere Désiré might throw off his constraints, his conditioning, and let himself go just a little, frolicking amid the ruins of his dogmas and the corpses of his masters, capering on his sinewy feet, hanging in mid-air from his shepherd's pipe? His dairymaid, with her milky shoulders, her lactescent breasts, her soft, creamy thighs, her buttery buttocks, is nothing other than a bit of cheesecake reincarnating Nisard's beloved wet nurse, a fine woman whose remarkable mammary hypertrophy—remarkable, albeit somewhat unwieldy for any activity not casting that majestic pair of breasts in a starring role—long occupied the whole of his consciousness, for the euphoric anticipation of the suckling to come gradually gave way, in the inhibited preadolescent's reveries, to visions of a less wholesome sort, and his sexuality remained forever marked by that mingling: all his life, Désiré Nisard was convinced that the man ejaculated the sweet, nourishing milk he had previously drunk from his lover's teat, and only with great difficulty did his mistresses disengage the ravenous customer so feverishly kneading and mouthing their breasts. Since Nisard did indeed end up expelling a few quarter-teaspoons of seed, he remained wholly convinced that this latter circulated from the woman to the man and then from the man to the woman, and nothing could shake that conviction, nor dispel his secret dread of the day when womankind, having perfected the system of pumps and tubes by which to procreate without the burden of the sexual act, would promptly eject the hairy-backed, yellow-footed male from the bed he crawled into eons before, and never left since. And since many a streetwalker showed him the door the moment he began pawing her in his own special way, he often concluded that the device had been made operational at last, and that he would never again know the dizzying raptures of love. Whereupon he boarded the first coach bound for Châtillon-sur-Seine, weeping all the way, and ran to nestle once more between his nurse's formidable breasts, after overcoming her initial resistance. Whence *A Milkmaid Succumbs*. As you see, this book's dismal enigmas can easily be solved without recourse to the volume itself; given this, we'd just as soon not delve into the details of the plot, wouldn't you agree?

For another, it is to be lamented that the lucidity which moved Nisard to seek out and destroy every last copy of his roguish tale did not shine its cold, objective light on his entire existence: a noose is so easily tied. He could have devoted that same persistence to expunging every last trace of his being, taking pains to leave nothing behind that might evoke him in mankind's memory, burning any register where his name had been scrawled, making liberal use of erasers and matches, eliminating every witness of his sojourn on earth, one by one, teachers, cousins, neighbors, landlords and landladies, in short performing the thankless task that today falls to me—I have so many better things to do! The example of *A Milkmaid Succumbs* proves it: who was better placed than Nisard to demolish Nisard, who more ideally suited for such a feat? Enlightened by this experience, and weary of continually retracing his steps to redress his wrongs, to withdraw his words and renounce his unfortunate initiatives, he would have given up acting, moving, speaking, in the end he would have given up living, granting posterity's fondest wish in his own lifetime, thereby sparing me the chore of destroying him myself, for which I would have given him a quick nod of gratitude, directed—in my inability to perceive its vanquished addressee—to the wind, to the leaves, to the otherworldly beauty of the world without Nisard.

What did this guy ever do to you, anyway? asks Métilde, who's never seen me so worked up, and who wishes I would massage her scalp just a little more gently, maybe quit pulling my hair, it's not very pleasant. You ask what he did to me? Surely, Métilde, you don't believe that the delicate fabric of days meted out to humanity for the embroidering of our adventures here on earth can survive undamaged when a being as ponderous as Nisard lolls upon it. Even today, we're still suffering the consequences of his baneful existence. Is he not, for example, the very cause of the brutality you've just chided me for? Métilde gives a nod, gingerly removing her head from my grasp.

GAP (AP) – *Caught in the act of burglarizing a clothing shop last September in Gap (Hautes-Alpes), a thief who had attempted to elude detection by posing as a store mannequin was sentenced Thursday evening by that city's criminal court to six months in prison, suspended, and a fine of 450 euros.*

Inebriated at the time of the incident, Désiré N. was quickly apprehended by officers, as he was unable to stand motionless for more than a few moments, and was furthermore dressed in clothes that had long gone out of style.

Finesse is certainly not Nisard's strong suit, his every act reveals an oafish sort of sensibility, and even if his desk-bound elbows were more callused than his palms, his fingers surely discerned no difference between a string and a steel cable. A lumbering character, crude, brutish, and proud of it, his boorishness on permanent display: one foot trampling a snail, the other a daisy, that's Nisard making his way through this world. Hark to his refrain: "*The source of a Golden Age's glory, and of its great men's enduring popularity, is that, having erected monuments of pure reason, they escape imagination's caprices. They are immortal because they are founded in human reason, which is immutable; they are inescapable because no intellectual order can exist without their example, just as no material order can exist without laws."*

Things are (what they are). Let us thank the poet who reveals this truth, and let us now ourselves recite the poem of the real in turn: there is a great deal of calcium in parsley. We must resign ourselves to that fact. You can cut your parsley in four, chop it fine, you will have changed nothing. Parsley is a plant rich in minerals. One might perhaps dream that things could be different. Better, however, to reserve our dreams for more realistic reforms, lest rude awakenings ensue. You will never dislodge the calcium from parsley. Never. It will not be moved. It's there to stay. There is a great deal of calcium in parsley, that statement brooks no contradiction. No disputing it, not even in the meekest murmur: you might as well pound at a wall till your fists are all bloody and bruised. The question is not up for discussion. Your thoughts on the matter are of interest to no one, and your howls of protest blow away on the wind. Your prayers will not be answered. The situation is at an impasse, nothing to be done. That calcium can also be found in almonds or endive comes as no consolation. We might wonder if it does not in fact compound our despair. Are we condemned to endure this forever? Apparently so. I roll a sprig of parsley between thumb and index finger, I crush it, I grind it, soon a damp wisp of green is all that remains: not a jot less calcium than before. An immoveable mountain, such is the calcium in parsley. An impregnable wall. An army would be powerless against it. Let us thus learn to rejoice in it. Let us love our masters. Hallelujah! Long live calcium! Long live parsley! Long live the calcium in parsley!

Monsieur and Madame Nisard named their son Désiré—unfortunately for him, as from that moment on he bears the name Désiré Nisard. For administrative purposes, he is Désiré Nisard. But it is also to this name that he must respond when hailed in the street. "Hey! There's Désiré Nisard!" say his acquaintances on seeing him draw near (but never on seeing Marc Palémon drawing near, or Albert Moindre, to cite only those two). Nor might he introduce himself under any other identity. He would be lying. He would forthwith be suspected of plotting who knows what manner of mischief. Those who speak of him among themselves never call him by any other name, any name other than Désiré Nisard: no doubt they'd rather say "Charles Baudelaire" or "Jules Barbey d'Aurevilly," but they can't. Désiré Nisard: that tells us who we're dealing with, that name on that face. Were he called André Dugas, for example, or merely Grégoire Reboul, it would be harder to get a handle on him. I myself briefly thought of christening him Forcinal, but I had to abandon that plan, for fear of misunderstandings and confusion. His morning mail comes to him marked with that same name, Désiré Nisard, inexorably. On hearing those five syllables, he reflexively raises his head. Often he then finds himself facing a person he knows. Almost always, in fact. He sometimes wishes he could answer to Boris Lelarge, or else, more secretly, perhaps blushing a little, Lorette Rossignol or Mirabelle Pam. But who would ever think of naming Désiré Nisard thus? He himself can only agree, gazing into his mirror each morning. Like it or not, the individual before him is none other than the one they call Désiré Nisard, incontestably.

But if he takes some manner of pleasure in this, if for some reason he thanks his lucky stars, well I'm sorry, but I don't, I can't come to terms with it, and I never will. That curse must be broken. Shake off that yoke, thrust your head out of that sack. Man has limped ever since Désiré Nisard first pulled on his boots. He piles error upon error. On average, at any given moment, four fingers out of five in this world are stuffed up somewhere they don't belong. Disastrous collapses soon follow, the dust rises into the sky, mud forms in the clouds and rains down in wads on the denizens of the crumbling cities. Helpless demographers observe a disturbing slump in the birth rate and yet a dizzying rise in the population, while the canniest climatologists house their families in shelters built to withstand both the tidal waves caused by the Earth's unstoppable warming and the bitter cold of the new ice age occasioned by the sun's coming extinction. That's where we stand. Oh, the harm Désiré Nisard has done us! His caviling, sermonizing, go-clean-your-room pronouncements have plunged us into this chaos more surely than all the orders to slash and destroy that have sprung from barbarous breasts since the dawn of civilization.

In the midst of magicians and sorcerers, Nisard is the disenchanter. Do you hear his imperturbable ticktock whenever happiness pays you its little annual call? No sooner have you finished building your nest than his saw digs into the tree trunk. His toenails are gimlets, and here he is boarding your boat. One end of your hammock is tied to a vigorous oak's stoutest branch, the other to a blade of grass lazily clamped between Nisard's gnawing teeth. From here on you'll have to drive on three wheels, the fourth is Nisard. He is the mouse to your cheese, the cat to your mouse, the dog to your cat, the truck that runs over your dog— and then what better name for the curve where your truck flies off the road? Here is the sad litany of the world-with-Nisard. At one moment or another, ineluctably, he shows up, a fossil bent on affecting the course of evolution once more, on intervening anew, on diverting the march of emancipation and progress, and Louis XIV will be the newly restored leader of the great apes. A dowser who'll never find a spring save to water the lawns of Versailles, that's Nisard.

Keep your cool, I exhort myself, bide your time. I stand facing Nisard, my two feet firmly planted. I eye him coldly. But I cannot confine him within my gaze, he escapes me on the right, on the left, all I can see is his nose, a sinister sight. His nostrils flare then clench, never did he so clearly articulate the principles of his finicky philosophy. His lips pronounce them more limply: engaged in a private chat on the reproduction of slugs, it always seems. If I turn my attention to his foot, wide and flat as a plinth, lumpy as a root, my affliction only deepens: how to cut the bolts on a statue that's also a tree? My gaze creeps up his two twisted legs, the pillars of the nineteenth century's foremost Greco-Roman temple. Where literature's concerned, I strongly disagree, but as for architecture, faced with this evidence, we can only concede its tragic decline. Inside his black trousers, Nisard's member makes a benign little lump that might nonetheless well be the tumor that does this world in. Nisard's arms reach out to embrace the void, he holds it close to his hollow breast; his fingers play over a rosary, the abacus of lost time. Finally my eyes roll back in my head (that reflex needs work: too slow).

What more might we learn from his contemporary Pierre Larousse? *A stout, almost globular body, covered in foul-smelling warts; short, stocky limbs; no teeth; two fatty glands under the neck; a muddy color; a clumsy gait; a pustular skin oozing a fetid, viscous, yellow liquid; red-tinged eyes: the toad might almost have been created to inspire a sort of repulsion.*

We dream of a book without Nisard. Which we would open like a window onto a world without Nisard, vast expanses without Nisard, not a shadow, not a footprint, it's a dream. We might follow a beautiful lady with a plaster cast on her wrist through the streets of Ulan Bator, or a turbulent little macaque from branch to branch, instead of which we must trudge, impatient and bored, through Désiré Nisard's interminable volume of *Travel Tales*: "*From Tarascon, I took the road to Marseille. Merciful heavens, what a road!*" He also took a steamboat down the

Rhône from Lyon to Arles. He saw Pau and Nîmes. He made a quick trip to Luxeuil. In London, he visited a pin factory and a madhouse on the same day—and there's a chapter right there. Then Désiré Nisard steers his bus into the streets of Westminster and Liverpool, expounding amid absolute silence, the passengers have all fallen asleep in their seats. Each time he stops in front of a church, a few more seize the opportunity to duck out. Soon he's alone, but on he drones all the same, evidently oblivious. In any case, taking up space is his only concern, filling his book with Nisard. Here he is in Belgium, then in Prussia, never missing a chance to be Nisard, Désiré Nisard, Jean-Marie-Napoléon-Désiré Nisard, shamelessly, with an absence of inhibition we find shocking today, but which provoked no particular outrage back then.

BREST (AP) – *A ship suspected of knowingly leaking oil at sea was sighted Friday morning off the coast of Brittany, trailing a slick 33 miles long and 44 yards wide, the Coast Guard office in Brest (Finistère) has reported.*

Carrying a cargo of perlite, the freighter was bound from Milos (Greece) to the Dutch port of Dordrecht when it was spotted by a customs surveillance plane some 70 miles west of the point of Penmarch (Finistère).

Authorities transmitted the evidence to the offices of the Public Prosecutor in Brest, which ordered the diversion of the 390-foot vessel. The freighter reached Brest in mid-afternoon, where, by order of the police, it was immediately boarded and impounded. Its

captain, Désiré N., was taken into custody and placed in preven-
tive detention.

Note the five fingers I have on each hand, out of which I can make
two balls worthy of Cassius Clay at the end of my scrawny arms.
My blood runs riot, it races through my veins, a tank car pulled by
four lathering horses. I grow. The function creates the organ: seriously, I'm sprouting muscles. Any moment now you risk a poke in
the eye from a button freshly popped off my short-sleeved shirt.
Do you hear that galloping sound? A herd of bison? It's my fingers, drumming on the table. The world trembles. A shiver runs
through the mountains, bowing the forests of larch. My every last
nerve burns to take part. Not one stands idly by. They rise up, they
bristle, yearning to bite and to sting. Those worms are hungry for
a corpse: there must be one around here somewhere. I'm following up on a very promising lead.

Have you seen that unctuous mug, that bovine snout, I want a
taste of that meat, I have the knife, the vinegar, all I need for a
quick little street-corner picnic. My every joint has become a jaw.
Nisard, you overripe cheese! You can't run from me, you're known
far and wide, even where fame has no name: your stench precedes
you. Oh, but it's true that a chair smashes when it's smashed! It's
true that, seized by the neck and smartly cracked against the bar,
any bottle becomes a crocodile's gaping maw: suddenly, before
me, a herd of fleeing gnus: Nisard. Beaming, the lamp invites me

to grasp its bludgeon of a base and strike yet again. From golf to guitar, it's all in the touch. My heart beats inside a gorilla's fist.

Métilde smiles in disbelief. She loved me for my unguents and balms, my caresses. Now contorted, I make a bewildering sight. Every seam of my garments is showing, every hem. No doubt my epidermis's red silk lining clashes a bit with the pallor familiar to my small circle of friends. Clearly no little girl named Luce or Adèle will come running to give me a hug this morning. I always did have a hardness inside me, and the shovel's sharp blade finally struck it, *clang*. Never again will I be dismembered with the butter wire. Désiré Nisard has awakened the brute in me, he fed it and armed it, the fool, and now he's goading it into action. What paltry use I've made of my bones until now! It's very simple, I made no use of them at all. Shoulder, elbow, knee: I never realized I was so well equipped. And yet see how easily my heel crushes, bashes, dispatches Nisard's frail frame. Nothing can resist it. So I really was walking on eggshells all this time! I throw punches left and right, my dogged rage runs right off to fetch back the stick. Its drool is a foaming potion that soothes my migraine. I make use of the buffalo's fearsome momentum, that mighty sprint had to lead somewhere: Nisard goes flying. All that blue above our heads is his beautiful bruise.

Then he falls on me again. It's as though we were bound by some giant rubber band. The more I shove him away, the more he comes back at me. And the mightier my thrust, the swifter his return. The greater my distance from Nisard, the tauter the band stretches, and sometimes, to my great shame, I'm the one abruptly lifted off the ground and launched toward Nisard, who thus sees me hurtling through space, flying toward him as if a lover's wings had sprouted from my back. We melt into a sickening, unnatural embrace, from which I struggle frantically to pull free, hamstrung by the tangled rubber band that now clasps us one to the other, knocked half senseless by his rancid breath, my movements slowed by his mucilaginous sweat: quick, before the glue dries and hardens, I've got to break loose. But the folds of his flesh are so many mouths hungrily pressed to my body—a sucking sound fills the air, a chewing, an absorbing, an assimilating: in the very nick of time, I tear myself away from that gummy embrace. For three days and three nights I run in a straight line, never glancing back; at long last I collapse into a weed-choked ditch, and merciful sleep carries me away farther still, to a place where my legs will never take me.

There are some whose leashed dog plays an indisputable part in their being, a sort of added value; they cannot be perceived—when they sit down on a café terrace, and the dog too, on its hindquarters, beside them—in isolation from that dog, severed from that dog, which, far from a mere accessory, a curly hairpiece or quadripedal prosthesis, modifies their person so entirely that it will bear the dog's stamp all its days, even in the absence of the dog, forever changed by the dog, unimaginable without the dog, the dog that is less an extension of their body than a component, acting on them like a chemical agent, transforming, no more no less, their molecular structure—often for the better, let us note, as the master-dog's skin now displays a new luster, his bearing a greater assurance, fitness, nobility, and this may be the most astonishing thing of all, for as it turns out the dog does not drag its master down into animality but rather confers on him an expanded human charisma, which must be why he burdens himself with the animal, though it is also true that not all comers will be identically modified by a dog of any given breed, susceptibility to these transformations varies from one human organism to the next, some even reject the dog outright, or take on precious few of its qualities, while others are more open to it, inviting the dog into them, shall we say, and there it frolics as freely as in any public park, rolling on the lawns, noisily slurping water from the fountain, and my fear, need it be said, is that Nisard will take possession of me in this very same way, through mimetism, impregnation, contagion, having so long clung to my heels, despite the kicks I continually inflict on his flanks and the cats I sew to his back, is that he will insidiously rework me, and that the very dodges and parries I perform to flee his irksome proximity might themselves refashion my form, that I might end up molding myself around his body's every protrusion, its every sordid protuberance.

And the more I dodge, duck, and buck, spurred by reflex, by repulsion, the more visible Nisard's loathed silhouette, ensconced at my side like an inseparable companion. This is his survival strategy. This is how he transcends the ages, despite his ineptitude.

The transparent jellyfish is revealed only by my allergy. My skin was smooth and white. His is red and raw. Such is my life, reduced to a perpetual bob and weave. Take away the bull, and the torero's arched back is ridiculous. That's why I point my finger at Nisard, that's why I call him by name. Doctor Zeller prefers to use such words as "deformation of the spinal column due to thoracolumbar kyphosis, with discal lesions and a deterioration of the cartilaginous growth plates of the vertebral bodies," then go on to prescribe twenty sessions of physical therapy. And how many sessions to resorb Islero, the steaming black Miura that gored Manolete at Linares on August 28, 1947?

Monsieur Nisard, writes Larousse, *then conceived a bold project: he would make of himself the past's ardent defender, and place the unruly schoolboys who dubbed themselves the Romantics once more under the pedagogue's heavy thumb. In a manifesto famous to this day, he divided literature into two camps: on the one hand easy literature, unbridled imagination run rampant, unworthy of occupying serious minds, and on the other difficult literature, whose far greater task is to imitate Boileau's* Epistles *or, at the very least, should inspiration fail, to translate Herodotus, Virgil, or Pliny. Jules Janin penned a very witty response to this pedantic absurdity, and with this Monsieur Nisard's name was made.* Sometimes a great sadness wells up inside me, like a wave, like nausea, and it's because there has been Nisard, because there is Nisard.

He is the slime at the bottom of every fountain. Irretrievably, there has been Nisard. How can we love benches, knowing that Nisard often pressed them into service? Gently stroking a cat's silken fur, my hand inevitably reproduces a gesture once made by Nisard. Strawberries are the less delectable for Nisard's love of them. I would welcome the immediate snuffing out of the beneficent sun that also warmed Nisard—sharing his filthy bathwater would inspire no greater disgust. If he could be besotted with a certain Élisabeth, how can we not be put off by the passions of love? Our innocence forever blushes at his brutish experience of this world. Nisard ruined everything in his wake, cities and countrysides alike. If he one day bit into a hazelnut, how can we still have a soft spot for squirrels? He was cold, he was hungry, whence we find those sensations so unpleasant today. Did Nisard ever make one single move that we might want to follow or imitate? Did he ever incarnate anything other than the tedium of being Désiré Nisard, definitively, forever and ever?

Strange but True

More than a hundred competitors from all over the world are slated to take part in a long-distance winkle-spitting contest tomorrow in Brittany. Last year's competition saw the world record of 32 feet shattered by Désiré Nisard, with a shot measuring 34 feet and 4 inches. The reigning champion has spent the past week in training, getting in "a few good spits every day" in hopes of "making it a little farther this year." While "a strong pair of lungs" is an indispensable asset, organizer Sophie Horviller recommends "making sure you turn the winkle around in your mouth so the pointed end comes out first, not the hole." (*Ouest-France*)

Nothing we learn of him fails to dismay us. Does some imbecility need to be uttered? Present! bellows Nisard, stepping forward. As a rake gathers leaves, his teeth scrape up all the withered ideas that litter the pathways of French gardens where no one ever strolls except in measured little steps, pontificating on ideas they know nothing about. On feeling a sudden surge of joy, he hops merrily around the begonia beds, from then on confined behind rows of low metal hoops: thus does this killjoy exult. Everything Nisard approaches warps, fades, cracks up. Fruits go rotten. Water is no longer suitable for drinking or bathing. Suddenly the thought that there has been Nisard, that there is Nisard, digs into us like a knife between two ribs, unerringly piercing the heart. There we were, serene and relaxed, and suddenly the memory of Nisard jabs into our brains like a spike, suddenly a spark from the bonfire ignites the dancing girl's delicate veil, and now we'll never be carefree again.

There we were admiring the griffon vulture, the monk vulture, the dwarf vulture, the gray vulture, the Egyptian vulture, the white-headed vulture, the Moluccan vulture, the helmeted vulture, the cinerous vulture, the green Goan vulture, the king vulture, the rock and limbo vulture, the gray-rumped vulture, the Mandarin vulture, the collared vulture, the crimson-bellied vulture, the wood vulture, the crested vulture, the chimera vulture, the snow vulture, the nutcracker vulture, the swimming vulture, the spotted vulture, the Saint-Jacques vulture, the horned vulture, the pilgrim vulture, the spiny vulture, the dropleted vulture, the placental vulture, the spangled vulture, the humming vulture, the garter vulture, the pink vulture, the lacy vulture, the abolitionist vulture, the tufted vulture, the saddled vulture, the pocket vulture, the weaver vulture, the blue vulture, the northern mocking vulture, the cloisonné vulture, the tomato vulture, the lyre vulture, the aposematic vulture, the nocturnal vulture, the bearded vulture, the smooth vulture, the pecking vulture, the moon vulture, the clown vulture, the mud vulture, the glass vulture, the bean-and-pea-seed vulture, the burrowing vulture, the granitic vulture, the rattle vulture, the leaf vulture, the pedipalpous vulture, the redpoll vulture, the reticulated vulture, the velvet vulture, the rockhopper vulture, the goat-headed vulture, the sage vulture, the chrysemys vulture, the chimney vulture, the twin vulture, the buff-spotted vulture, the red-shouldered vulture, and all those birds are so lovely, so magnificent, that we naïvely forgot their bloodthirsty hunger for flesh; and then the common or gutter vulture, circling above us, fixes its crosshairs on our skulls, and our memory returns.

"There is no finer way to arrive in Arles than on a steamboat descending the Rhône," Désiré Nisard writes, for example, since I must after all offer my reader a taste of his work, however it pains me, that the cause of my wrath be fully understood. I believe this citation can stand on its own, without further comment. Just take

a moment and consider the inanity of that prose, how it bores, how it bogs, how utterly it fails to transport us, for all its exertions: rightly doubting his powers, the pitiable Nisard thought it necessary to requisition a steamboat! And even with that, the proclamation remains entirely without interest. We're all free to go to Arles—*à Arles*, as he puts it—however we please, and should we lose our way en route some helpful farmer or villager will surely point us in the right direction. Clearly, we have a more elevated idea of literature than Jean-Marie-Napoléon-Désiré Nisard, we seek from it something more than mere itineraries. To our minds, the published works of Monsieur Michelin do not figure among literature's major triumphs; a very fine opening scene, the world as if laid out before our eyes, then nothing more. Might I also, without priggish pedantry, remind Nisard that one says *en* Arles, and not *à* Arles, and suggest to him that the fine French language of the seventeenth century might have declined so precipitously only because it was entrusted to so slovenly a custodian? Whose last choking gasp, as it happens, we hear in *à Arles*. Finally, let us note how archaic that style of his now seems, and how little of value remains of that stale preachment: we would be most hard-pressed today to locate a steamboat on which to descend the Rhône. A truly significant work of literature, on the other hand, never loses its pertinence.

"*The Rhône is the natural avenue from Lyon to the enchanting city of Arles*," Désiré Nisard also writes, Nisard whom I here cite once more, for it would perhaps be unjust to judge him by one single sentence. The objective reader is first struck by the extreme thematic poverty of Nisard's notion of literature. There is a near-pathological fixation here, which certainly explains many things. Any author who strays ever so slightly from that natural avenue is immediately disgraced in Nisard's benighted mind. For him, the writer's range of actions and interventions must be narrowly de-limited: a particularly daring author might set out to defend that means of locomotion against all the rest. Coming as it does prior to the invention of the dirigible, the automobile, the train, and the airplane, his bold position on steamboats was in the end vexing only to horses. Even today, if you stand before a horse and shout Nisard's name square in its nostrils, it will knock off your straw hat and eat it without further ado.

Suppose you wrote me a poem? Métilde suggests. I see what she's up to: she wants me to calm down. Or maybe take a walk in the garden? she says. Really, I sometimes think she has no idea what's going on here. Is she pretending? Is it a virtue to go through life as if Nisard never was, or as if we were now permanently delivered of that torment? One can blind oneself to certain things, but who can distract us from the knife tunneling into our entrails? Métil-de's insouciance arouses now my admiration, now my wrath. And then I wonder if that insouciance is not in fact the highest form of contempt. A sovereign disdain: for her, it is indeed as if Nisard never existed. The day Désiré Nisard was to have been conceived, Nisard *père* found himself obliged to spend the night in Paris, or perhaps a migraine-racked Nisard *mère* spurned his advances.

Such is Métilde's disdain that the Nisard couple's uninspired co-itus is abruptly interrupted by the outbreak of a fire in the conjugal bedroom, or the intrusion of a bat by way of the window. Depleted by frequent masturbation, Nisard *père* proves incapable of honoring his spouse. That morning, Nisard *mère* packed her bags and fled to Calais and her waiting lover, a young infantry lieutenant; now she's sailing for England: such is Métilde's disdain for Nisard. Nisard *père's* semen winds up harmlessly in Nisard *mère's* mouth. Six months pregnant, the poor woman takes a nasty fall in the street. But in 1808 she will deliver her first son, Charles, and the following year she'll give birth to the rector of the Académie de Grenoble, Auguste; two fine boys, of sturdy constitution, thanks to whom she will soon forget that unfortunate incident. Such is Métilde's disdain for Nisard.

Literary Trivia
Who said: "*Go and see Arles, all you who love the arts; and by all means travel there by way of the Rhône*"?

My laughter's finally broken free of its shackles, do you hear? And it's neither nightingale trills in the enraptured azure nor tinkling goat bells in Alpine pastures: rather, the distinctive staccato produced by the vertebrae of a certain French critic as he clatters down his staircase like a runaway funicular. My laughter is ringing: pick up. Hear what it has to say. All that glass couldn't go on standing forever perched on one foot, nor the river forever follow its banks. Nor the tree stay forever rooted to its spot, standing by: your wait is over, I've learned to make matches. I know how to feed geese through a funnel: thus will my laughter force its way between your pinched lips. My laugh is expansive and sonorous. Baby teeth, rotten teeth: in that laugh they're all still in place, firmly implanted, not one is missing, suddenly it's somewhere else that gaps, cracks, and mutilations appear. Everything is hollow for my laughter, that's what I've discovered, it penetrates the densest stone, and will shatter it when I decide the hour has come.

It won't be long. I've run through my stores of patience, indulgence, accommodation. I'm all out of tears. I'll have to migrate toward some other water source. And soon they'll flow elsewhere: that's a threat. I've bayoneted too many sandbags, my place is like a desert. Visitors lost in the dunes are thoughtfully prodded back to the path by a scorpion. I've contained myself for too long. With ever greater difficulty, however, and ever more lapses. It was yawning that gave me away, I was forever having to choke back my elbows, I didn't always land on my feet. Enough of this politic body! Only a porcelain elephant prudently sticks to the threshold of its little shop. If I could just let myself go once and for all, I'd find ways of dealing with Nisard. And as I await that deliverance, I militate, I recruit, I convert. No flame performs a single tawny, fluid undulation that it did not learn from my example in that night class, also attended by the cobra. I rouse the tiger, resting too comfortably on its age-old reflexes, as if roaring and leaping were enough nowadays! We're readying its big comeback: it's got some surprises in store. I have this piece of advice for the shark, always well intentioned but short on sound guidance: let the lighthouses and buoys show you the way. The tarantula was lost too, poor little thing, in the dark Amazonian forest. I'm clearing her a path to Nisard, ripping out tree trunks, toppling walls. A colossal upraised middle finger on a bulldozer's prow, the rhinoceros now precedes me and represents me all over the world. I have a message for Nisard. The rhino will see it gets through.

ALICANTE (AP) – *There were no miracles Sunday on the clay court in the bullring of Alicante. With Désiré Nisard's unceremonious defeat at the hands of Rafael Nadal, 6-4, 6-1, 6-2, Spain has knocked France out of the Davis Cup semifinals.*

Drafted in at the last minute to replace an injured Carlos Moya, Nadal, only 18, left no opening for a sluggish Nisard, who never fully engaged in the match and offered his youthful opponent no real challenge. The selection of Désiré Nisard, who was eliminated in the first round of each of this year's four Grand Slam tournaments, caused some grumbling in the ranks of the French Tennis Federation; Sunday evening in Alicante, team captain Guy Forget publicly regretted his choice. "Nisard is no longer on the team," he concluded.

France withdraws from the competition without glory.

Great is the sorrow of knowing that Nisard has weighed so heavy on the ways of this world, that he is the origin of an endless chain of consequences whose cogwheels are still turning today, those gears crush everything they snatch up in their teeth, relentless rustproof mechanisms interlocking one with the next and covering the world with their clamor, laminating, mowing, twisting, compressing—and then, when we look up from the incomprehensible labors assigned us, we catch sight of our faces reflected in an oncoming warhead. What's the name of the manufacturer of fast-acting poisons and slow-working pollutions that employs us? *Nisard and Co.*, what else? Is there one single spot on this earth unravaged by his nefarious influence? Out on the ice floe, see that worrisome crack racing along beneath your feet, zigging and zagging, branching in every direction. The desert's shifting sands finish the jobs left undone by that dreamer: burials, suffocations . . . Where to flee? Is the dream of a world without Nisard mere fantasy? Not only are you deep in the hole, but you're there with Nisard. And is it worth trying to scale the summits, knowing that there too the only view is Nisard, Nisard as far as the eye can see, unless you turn your gaze to the heavens?

I suspect that he sometimes slips into our shoes. No choice but to walk on and endure the discomfort, or you'll slow down the whole group. Your foot is rubbed raw. At last the hikers pause for a break and you pull off your boot. A tiny pebble falls into your hand. Perhaps a mere grain of sand. The fishbone, the splinter, the rock-hard pit, that was him. That was Nisard. And it is him too that I blame for all our pettiest misfortunes, minor mishaps that would mean nothing if they occurred in a life filled with joy, but which always materialize against a background of sorrow and so grind down our resistance, our patience, all the forces we've marshaled to struggle against a malevolent fate.

In the Offices of Doctor Nisard

So much metal in my body, so many steel plates, screws, pins, rivets: I sometimes feel I'm one with my wheelchair, its wheels spinning on an axis thrust through my waist. So twisted a body, frozen in an impossible pose that not even the limberest gymnast could hold for ten seconds, despite the applause of the spellbound crowd. My ribcage is a tangle of bones, my shoulders nestle one against the other, left to right, like a couple entwined, making their way toward a still closer embrace.

"Glasses! From now on, you'll have to wear glasses."

The voice you hear is that of Doctor Nisard, ophthalmologist. He's just examined my eyes. Irrefutably, my vision is dimming. I'm going to need glasses. Nothing to do, however, with the accident that folded me into this wheelchair a few years ago. This time it's genetic. It's in my blood. This time, black ice is not to blame. And then that wall suddenly popping up in front of me. Not this time, no. This affliction comes courtesy of my father or mother. Nothing serious, of course. All the same, it has to be corrected before it gets worse.

"Glasses! What you need is a good pair of glasses, you'll see."

What's in there, do you think, clasped in the grip of my stitched-up skin? You can't figure it out. Did this membrane perhaps grow around a table, or a wheelbarrow, or what? What sort of skeleton makes such odd angles? Men aren't supposed to have all these knees, all these elbows! Study me from this side, that side, you don't get it, not even with one eye closed or head cocked. Men aren't supposed to have all these dimples, not even when they laugh. Doctor Nisard jams the glasses onto my mangled face.

"Try and tell me I'm wrong."

My shoulder blades are like two cymbals: you expect at any moment to hear the glorious crash of their collision, the golden note that never comes, that might justify all of this, this whole horrible contortion. You'll never get used to it. My spinal column would not greatly hamper a snake in its sinuous slither. And indeed, a strident hiss continuously emanates from my choked larynx. It would seem that a slight back-and-forth motion of the upper body is the only movement still permitted me.

"So slight, in fact, that you're in no danger of losing your glasses."

So jokes Nisard. This face of mine, maimed in the accident, smashed, crumpled, then restored catch as catch can, remodeled as best they were able, will now be asked to hold a simple pair of glasses in place. One complication on top of another! My nose is no longer what it was, and as for my ears . . . My nose, you see, suddenly chose to set off in a new direction, and as for my ears, they underwent all manner of stitching, grafting, cauterizing, good luck wedging anything atop or behind them. My eyes themselves no longer line up as they do on a human face. They're so far apart. Which is the right, which the left?

"I have to tell you, you're not making this easy."

So all that wasn't enough. Something still missing. The finishing touch. They stepped back for a look, and evidently they still weren't quite satisfied. They stared at me, baffled. They scratched their heads. They bit their lips. Maddening. They could see it: I was close but not yet wholly submerged in the deepest possible misery. Yes, almost there—but what else? Should something be taken away? Added? They couldn't make up their minds. It was Nisard who came up with the answer.

"Glasses! We'll give him glasses."

(End of the consultation)

I have only one question for the surgeon: how does one flay a man? And for the mason: how does one wall up a man? For the fisherman: how does one harpoon a man? For the farmer: how does one harvest a man? For the executioner: how?

There's only one sure cure for cockroaches. Sprays and foggers pollute your home, and can moreover be toxic to delicate flour mites, to whom we mean absolutely no harm (Métilde went to Mali to pick up some sorghum flour just for them). The traps sold in shops—little stickum-lined boxes, glue-coated strips of wood—catch mostly dust, never again to dance in the rays of the sun, pity. No, what I recommend is a homemade poison with the simplest of recipes: a dose of boric acid stirred into sweetened condensed milk. This gives you a glutinous paste, which you then pour into saucers and set out in strategic locations: highly enticing to the cockroach's palate, the concoction renders it sterile. A few days later it dies, without descendents.

Stand solidly braced, knees flexed, feet flat on the ground, some distance apart. Point your index finger straight ahead at eye level toward your opponent, with your arm slightly bent. The cry has to come from the diaphragm. Tense your abdominal muscles, then relax just as it bursts from your mouth. All the strength you have in you must pass through your finger. That's how my karate manual describes the *kiai*, the cry that kills. I'm boning up. The *kiai*'s success, it also says, depends on the intensity of the cry—you can count on me—on the conviction invested in it—I won't let you down—on its perfect execution—it'll be flawless—and on the mental state of the enemy, whose focus must have a weak spot—no point going on, then, it won't work: Désiré Nisard is a granite block of hateful concentration, impervious to attack.

I've said it before, I'm hoping for a spontaneous outpouring of support to see this thing through. Were our world to come under alien attack, I like to think we earthlings would find it within ourselves to still our internal dissensions and unite against the common foe. It is just such a groundswell I'm calling for here. If the battle against Nisard could reconcile a strife-torn humanity, there would at least be that one justification for his noxious existence. At long last, we would witness the coming of one single man, composed of all mankind yet renouncing not one of man's innumerable faces, nor the endlessly varied facets of his thought, and that man would rise up and face Nisard. Imagine: we all stand together, arm in arm, melding into one single rank, and we advance on Nisard, who now finds himself alone, isolated, with only his own feeble resources to aid him, summoning from within himself only a few more spurts of saliva to spit at us. But his expectorations no longer reach us, they only dampen his feet. Inexorably, Nisard backs away. Behind him lies the firing wall. The sheer cliff. The dragon's lair. We advance. Nisard retreats. What a merry dance! That's how I picture the festivities. We advance. He retreats, backing over the gleaming parquet floor, the gay tones of our waistcoats and hoop skirts reflected in the polished wood. The music's a bit mincing, perhaps, but that's just the ticket today. Our children point their sharpened lollipops before them. Nisard retreats. He retreats, arms outstretched, begging for mercy. But no, we're going to demolish him, right?

Let him only speak, and every woman will immediately stand with me against him. "*I heard the word of consent,* ja, *yes, so sweet and so flattering in the mouth of that young German girl, a symbol of every woman's destiny, which is to consent,*" he says, for example, words sure to arouse that gender's fury, though likely, too, to raise an army of men suddenly eager to do battle for Nisard's cause. Even here we can see the torments that his vile, specious thinking visits upon this world. It's at work all around us. Nothing can stop it. The bone of the hardest skulls is the butter on its bread.

Shortly thereafter, under the Guizot ministry, Pierre Larousse continues, unflappable, *Monsieur Nisard was named senior lecturer at the École Normale (1835), then director of the Secretariat at the*

Ministry of Public Education (1836), then Counsel at the Conseil d'État (1837), then head of the Division of Sciences and Letters at the Ministry of Public Education (1838). In order to reach these heights, he had quelled his ardent Republican convictions; at the same time, eager to attract a man of this stature to their side, the Ministry chose to forget that he had once referred to Louis-Philippe as "the king of the June Days" and mocked the monarch's august portrait. All he lacked was a position as Ministerial deputy; that too was soon his. Elected to the Chambre des Députés by the district of Châtillon-sur-Seine, he served from 1842 to 1848, with no distinction whatever; this notwithstanding, he was chosen to succeed Burnouf as Professor of Eloquence at the Collège de France in 1844, proving that theory and practice are two very different things. Such, then, was Nisard's meteoric rise through the ranks of the State, fueled by his treachery and his fickleness. So thoroughly did he confuse his ambitions for France with his own private aspirations that he must have believed he was bringing comfort and joy to an entire people whenever he warmed his feet before the fire, a fine cigar between his lips. And if only Pope Pius IX had had the presence of mind to place a crown on his head in the Cathedral of Reims, then France would instantly have become the happiest, most prosperous nation on earth. *Désiré Nisard, or The Compleat Politician* was the title I long envisioned for the present hagiography, then I decided on *Demolishing Nisard*, which packs more of a punch.

PARIS (AP) – *In a Tuesday interview on RTL Radio, Désiré Nisard denounced the "excessive power" of examining magistrates and the press's insistence on bringing up the allegations being leveled against him, even as he basked in his reelection to the Chambre des Députés this past Sunday.*

"My opponents' attempts to take me down were a pure waste of time," declared Monsieur Nisard, named Representative for the district of Châtillon-sur-Seine in Sunday's elections. "It's a fact that the power given examining magistrates is excessive, and it's a fact that the system is a disaster," he added. "They come up with their own ideas, then look for evidence to confirm them: that has nothing to do with the proper course of justice."

Questioned at length about the investigations currently targeting him, Monsieur Nisard repeatedly refused to answer, asking the RTL journalist, "Are you an examining magistrate?"

Suspected of embezzlement, of multiple misappropriations of public funds, of misuse of company assets, of money-laundering, and most notably of dealing arms to the Angolan regime of Eduardo Dos Santos, the former director of the Secretariat at the Ministry of Public Education firmly denied that he had sought a seat in the Chambre des Députés only in order to acquire parliamentary immunity.

What a bastard! An elusive enemy, difficult to take out. Battling the hundred-headed hydra would be a picnic next to this. Because here the head is precisely nowhere to be found. Quite a dilemma for the valiant knight. He has to lash out blindly. The blow that finally lands will be a stroke of pure luck.

With which the old dream of a book without Nisard is reborn. To hear him tell it, this could only be some mawkish romance, some puerile inanity, enough of those foolish tales. Literature is no idle fantasy. The book without Nisard will be possible only in a world without Nisard. Alas, this world is Nisard's oyster, immunized as he is, mithridatized as he is against every conceivable poison, vaccine, insecticide, supremely resistant, supremely hardy, and, need it be said, supremely protected, enjoying the multiple complicities of allies both natural and opportunistic, of collaborators, acolytes, champions, and partisans, always ready to conceal him, feed him, perhaps die for him. He has hideouts everywhere, secret chambers, underground bunkers, fortified castles. His many look-alikes dine on meals identical to his own, to preserve their likeness with his grotesque physique. He travels in armored cars, and never leaves home without a stout escort of bodyguards extensively trained in blood sports. That vast organization reproduces Nisard's singularity beyond his own limits. His thought is the gray mortar that holds it all together. Thus, before anything else, we must reduce Nisard to silence. That's how we'll annihilate him. This book has no other ambition than to deprive Nisard of yet another space in which to promulgate his program. We've left the field open for him long enough. Let us publish where he was preparing to publish. Let us eat the paper he was hoping to cover with words. To be sure, this book is drenched in Nisard, but that excess, as must already be clear, has no other goal than to provoke the nausea that will deliver us of him at last, the cleansing regurgitation that is the healthy response of any organism under assault in its vital principle, and which, spectacularly, brings it relief. In order finally to read the book without Nisard—possible only in the world without Nisard—we must first pass through this book chock-full of Nisard, depending on that overabundance to arouse the purgative reflex that will at long last expel Nisard from this world forever.

I have to cram all of Nisard into this book, that he might in the end be ejected from it with one mighty blast, leaving no seed behind, no stump, no cluster of gelatinous eggs to doom my endeavor. I've set out to destroy Nisard, and my intention is most certainly not to give him a scolding, nor even a sound thrashing, nor to embellish his broad, pallid face with a shining black eye and empurpled nose: might as well man the pump that keeps his blood flowing! No, I want to erase the very memory of Nisard, down to the tiniest trace. Not reduce him to shards or powder: the wind would sprinkle those spores over some putrid soil where they would immediately put down roots. No seed scattered on the ground fails to find a womb in the end. Nisard has already annexed more than one uterus, more than one nest. That parasite would just as happily grow in a she-donkey's intestine. He would thrive in the spawn of an eel. Viviparous or oviparous, Nisard can be hatched by all; no one is safe. And it's always a painful delivery. No little episiotomy will spare you. Forty feet of thread for the post-natal suture, I've heard. Is there no hope of regaining the tranquility that reigned before procreation? Once there was nothing and then there was something, and as it happened this was a bad thing, for the result was Nisard.

My bronchial tubes are racked by spasms of the smooth muscle and a hypersecretion of mucus, whence the respiratory difficulties I complain of, diagnosed by the doctors as severe asthma. My sleep-disrupting sneezing fits and nasal congestion, on the other hand, they attribute to atopic rhinitis, and to a nasty case of conjunctivitis the unending flow of tears that anyone else might have blamed on my sorrow. My pruriginous lesions and the horrible itch they produce come from nettle rash, not my eczema, which for its part is the cause of the oozing pustules on my stomach, expertly distinguished by the dermatologist from the herpes, shingles, and lupus erythematosus that also afflict me. They fear for my life. My charts further allude to edema, hypertension, fever, pulmonary infiltrates, periarteritis nodosa, acute glomerulonephritis. Only one thing to be done, in all haste, say the doctors: identify the allergen.

Why get yourself in such a state? Métilde asks pityingly, as she cuts up my pills and mixes my ointments. Just laugh him off, she adds. But Nisard feeds on our jeers, they only refresh his complexion's greenish glow, and further fuel his destructive powers. To turn our backs on him is to give him the run of all the lands that lie behind us. And then when we want to come back to them, we'll find him there, firmly implanted—good luck chasing him off! Nisard's substance impregnates everything he touches, simply evicting him's not enough, you also have to sweep away his smell, disperse his miasma. How do you air out the world? Tainted, stinking fluids permeate the earth deep beneath his feet.

Don't expect much luxuriance from the springtime to come: a few swamp flowers, maybe . . . Nisard is a perpetual fountain of wastewater. Wherever he goes, he flows; he can saturate any soil—contemporary science knows no treatment for that toxic waste. I sometimes wonder if Nisard hasn't always been with us in this degenerated, decomposed state, or, more precisely, if this latter is not in fact his original state. Everything molds except *Stachybotrys atra*, the mold fungus, hardy and evergreen. Nisard's insolent good health flowers on the world's ailing body.

Proteases are enzymes that prove highly effective against stains left by egg, milk, blood, grass, and other organic protein-based soils; lipases attack oil and grease, lipstick, butter, cosmetics; amylases dissolve glucides and thus wash away stubborn traces of potato, cocoa, and pasta; cellulases break up the blot held captive in textile fibers by stripping away cellulose microfibrils. But what enzyme will act on the pollution Nisard leaves behind? No smudges of chocolate or strawberry in his wake. What solvent, what abrasive, what ultra-powerful detergent will wash away that filth?

Literature as Nisard sees it is a grim, gloomy missal, a lesson in resignation. The reader comes to it for sermons and reprimands, head bowed in penitence. On this score at least, duly chastised and chastened, Nisard could only have applauded the present volume. As he sees it, literature serves to promulgate the moral laws governing the human species. Writers are spiritual guides, directors of conscience. The lost soul will never consult them in vain, they will unfailingly steer him right. *"Take up a map and follow the course of the Rhône southward from Lyon. At the far end, where the river splits into two branches before rolling on toward the sea, you will discover a tiny black dot and a name in small letters: that is Arles."* Folly, fantasy, satire, bitter defiance, melancholy, and all the other black suns of poetry have tumbled into the ditch along with the top-heavy milkmaid. There remains only, planted by the roadside, a scowling scarecrow coiffed with a bishop's miter: literature as Nisard sees it.

Whence came this radical notion? In the wake of what studies, after what long sleepless nights, how did Désiré Nisard forge this idea of literature, in what forge? We might posit some cruel experience of the fragility of things, of the faithlessness of women, instilling in him a certain taste for rigor. We know, too, of the fascination exerted on weak personalities by military discipline and the arrogance of religion. Was it just such a complex that fostered the germination and growth of Nisard's austere theories? We would have liked to know the circumstances of his first encounter with literature, the context of that revelation, and what manner of life, wholly devoted to that passion for the written word, he led from then on. Nisard once touched on this, with some candor, in an account of his travels in England: *"In order to occupy my evenings and rainy days, I had brought with me a Homer and a La Fontaine. The weather proved unusually damp, and so I had every occasion to read those two peerless poets."* To be sure, I feel no fondness for Nisard, that grim forerunner of our era's most disheartening missteps, but my jaw can only drop in awe when I consider his breathtaking foresight, for he truly was a man ahead of his time: fully one hundred years before the televisual age, was Nisard, snug in his London flat, his volumes open before him, not inventing the inert TV viewer?

Force-feed him pebbles. Drive a nail into his eye. Fray the skin on his ankles. Polish a six-sided paving stone against his head. Promise him something and don't follow through. Push him out of the airplane. Spray herbicide on his golf course. Sell him for his pelt to a blind taxidermist. Sink his boat. Bleed into his milk. Laugh at his sorrows. Stuff his potbelly with jingle bells. Empty his tubes and jars. Disperse his collections. Equip his moles and ferrets with the requisite tools. Bombard his homestead. Shorten his trouser legs. Call him a sheath in front of a swordsman seeking a place to stow his weapon. Starve his tiger. (*Further suggestions welcome*)

A pastime for rainy days, that's what Homer is for Nisard. It's raining outside, nothing better to do, let's read Homer. And yet credible witnesses tell of Nisard racing out the door when the first drops began to fall, a basket over one arm, to gather meadow mushrooms or hunt the tender, creamy snails of his native Burgundy— is that little outing what he calls *The Odyssey*? In summertime, then, Nisard read even less, counting on the occasional shower to refresh his erudition, but choosing only the most arid regions for his holidays: because reading is such a tedious thing, after all. But it must be said, in all fairness, that even on dry days Nisard could sometimes be found with his nose in a book, visibly mesmerized. That book being the *National Meteorological Survey*, with which he was carefully plotting his upcoming vacation's itinerary by the average rainfall of each department of France: because reading is such a chore, after all. Nisard vastly prefers gamboling through the heather or knocking the seedheads off wild grasses with a brisk swipe of his walking stick. Nisard would rather roll in the sawdust. He'd rather rub his back against the rugged bark of great pines. Oh, how he would rather putter with the muskrat in the tall grass, or take potshots at the white butterflies of the fields, aiming for the black spots on their wings.

Nisard reads a few lines here and there once the showery season starts up. But what a thankless task is reading, and what a waste of time when there's no rain in the air! Should we then infer that Désiré Nisard is a man of bright, sunny temperament? Should we conclude that Nisard is a man with a hearty appetite for life, lustily sinking his teeth into every available pleasure? Yes, but only in the manner of the alligator—and then he drags his victim down into the murky depths. Whatever Nisard touches, he degrades beyond repair. Literature never recovered from that encounter. The warbler will no longer sit on its eggs, now impregnated with his scent, and it's the same for every living thing on this earth. No downy, protective wing now warms this infected world, but the orbiting vulture's need no longer even flap to hold it aloft over the devastated hills and dales: little by little, above our heads, the circles of its fateful trajectory grow ever tighter.

Nisard plucks apples all the more easily in that the apple tree wants nothing more to do with any apple Nisard has touched. The apple tree releases the apple into the hollow of his cupped hand. The apple tree abandons her apple to him. The apple tree spits the core, the seeds, the skin, and all the applesauce straight into Nisard's ugly mug. All the apples from the apple tree crash down on Nisard. Pears fall no less mysteriously, and plums, onto Nisard's shoulders and back, and the formidable coconut, designed for this very purpose, knocks him flat. Chestnut tree, what are you waiting for? The right moment, comes the reply, and then it's a hail of sharp, well-aimed blows that suddenly pepper Nisard's tortured body. There's the smooth, dense, round chestnut, which is a mighty fist. And the chestnut still in its burr, which delivers more of a slash, like a clawed foot. We have need of them both, working as one: then we'll have some chance of getting the better of Nisard.

Who would have thought it? So the meadow mushroom was poisonous, so the Burgundy snail was venomous! Oh joy!

It was in a carefree mood that Désiré Nisard set off on his walk last Tuesday afternoon: with his four dogs by his side, he thought he had nothing to fear. He was thus ambling at a leisurely pace through the woods of Courcelles-Frémoy—when suddenly a wild boar burst from a thicket. The son of an avid hunter, Monsieur Nisard recognized the beast as a male of some 150 pounds. His first thought was for his dogs' safety, but all at once the boar wheeled with a grunt and charged straight at him, violently butting him before fleeing into the forest. Despite the shock and a nasty wound to the arm, Désiré Nisard made his way unaided to the hospital of Semur, where he was given some ten stitches. The "pig," as such creatures are called in these parts, inspires no small terror in men: strong and powerfully built, it seems to know no fear, and when threatened hurtles straight ahead at full speed. Nonetheless, explains veterinarian Yves Pelleport, the wild boar is highly reluctant to attack, and does so only when it has no other choice. Here I simply transcribe, unembellished, an article published in this morning's issue of *Le Bien Public*, but these words fully express the regrettable necessity that is indeed mine. I would be more than happy to wear down my incisors only by rooting for juicy larvae and succulent roots, and to saunter serenely through the wheat fields rather than redden my pelt with Nisard's bloodied flesh. Nature did not endow me with a radar-fine snout for the purpose of sniffing out that gentleman, and besides, let it be said once and for all, even if I do someday succeed in making mincemeat out of him, my mouth will always water more abundantly before a nice dish of puréed chestnuts.

I charge without fear, head down, my body a solid block behind my massive parietal bone, but my attacks never bear fruit. Once again, Nisard emerges unscathed. I have a proposition to submit to the local town council. I'm a citizen here, after all. They will surely see fit, or so I hope, to place this request on their next meeting's agenda: why not introduce buffalo into the woods of Courcelles-Frémoy? There's no other way, Monsieur Pelleport has conceded as much, mere flight is pointless and leads nowhere; for too long our policy has been one of avoidance, evasion, and look where it's got us. Because now we're surrounded, and to make matters worse the enemy enjoys the aid of accomplices within our own camp, can anyone seriously doubt it? Anyone who did seriously doubt it would immediately be taken for the traitor himself, and quite right too. Nisard invades us, infects us. We have no other choice, Pelleport agrees: we've got to demolish him.

Nisard sings, and stones rain down on the schools. He dances, and all the gold underground turns to lead. Plants that once climbed now creep low to the ground, fleeing the sound of his laughter. In the dead of winter, he breaks an old woman's window to fill a blind beggar's cup with glass shards. He uses his phone on trains. He revs his engine in quiet streets. He is the noisy neighbor to the right of his neighbor to the left and the noisy neighbor upstairs of his neighbor downstairs and the noisy neighbor to the left of his neighbor to the right and the noisy neighbor downstairs of his neighbor upstairs. He writes appallingly bad books. He dips his big fat feet in the sea.

And yet just this morning, no lie, I thought it had finally happened, come to pass at long last: the world without Nisard. Métilde had gathered her hair into one single tress, contained in her delicate hand. With a supple flip of the wrist she tossed it on top of her head, where it formed a suspended nest, promptly affixed with a barrette to her auburn locks, in which no bird has yet thought wise to settle: it's one thing to soar high over the mountaintops, quite another to sit perched on the head of a skipping, lighthearted girl. I shouldn't have trusted the strange rush of euphoria that had me, too, feeling so buoyant, where morning usually finds me so weighed down, so inert. Ah, but here's the thing, a summit exists only by virtue of the abyss that surrounds it. Exultation is only a rocket shooting into a leaden sky. I reached out to grasp the wonders revealed in the revitalized light of that first morning without Nisard, and my hand met only emptiness. Will the beauty of things, then, remain forever impalpable, abstract, the stuff of legend or hallucination, such that we will never feel our own existence but by grasping whatever we can catch—chills, crabs—whatever is hard, oppressive, sharp, with nothing more to look forward to than those handfuls of pain or disappointment? And so Nisard reappears yet again, summoned up by my own terror of death and disintegration, because nothing is tangible other than him, and because I myself prefer his brutality to the impalpable mist of my rose-tinted longings.

No, no, I won't let myself say that. *Get Out, I'm Coming In*—that too could be the title of this work conceived as an instruction manual for the elimination of Désiré Nisard. But must we be sucked up by the vacuum he vanishes into? No: we'll inhabit that vacuum as free men, unfettered by any one incarnation resulting from chance and biology. No more, in that emancipated existence, will our scores be definitively settled at birth. The end of Nisard will mark the dawn of a new era for a humanity weary of groping its way through the night: for night has enveloped us from the start, who can doubt it? Nisard was the first aquatic mutant to equip himself with feet, so as to clamber out of the protozoan swimming pool and impose his law on dry land. When man hoisted himself onto the banks in his turn, little livelier than a drowned body washed up by the tide, shivering and naked, ashamed of his pink, descaled sex, it was too late: Nisard already reigned. We will live our lives in meek apprehension, perpetually fearing his wrath. The child will be born in terror, and there he'll stay until the moment of his death, his final horror. He who would rebel, by word or by deed, will be punished without mercy. Arteries blocked off by the police, his blood screeches to a halt. He is thrown to earth and brutalized. Nisard's got us just where he wants us: he knows what school our little girls go to, and he tells us so with a sinister leer. He owns the four walls we live between, and can toss us out into the street whenever he chooses. He holds the world economy in his hands, shamelessly favoring those who flatter him and toil to expand his power. Above all, he uttered the first principle of logic, and we've been chained to its train of consequences ever since.

The Bible has its biases, its fits of temper; the legal code too has its pets and its pariahs; the true book of wisdom is the dictionary. Larousse continues as follows: *Between those two dates, Monsieur Nisard published a* History and Description of the City of Nîmes *(1835, in-octavo), planned as part of an ambitious collection on the cities of France, and a volume of* Collected Essays, *containing accounts of his travels, fragments of literary history, and criticism (1838, in-octavo); he further put his name to a bilingual edition of the Latin classics,* A Collection of Latin Authors, with Translations, Published under the Direction of Monsieur D. Nisard *(1838–1850, 27 volumes, royal octavo). All the while, from his chair at the Collège de France, Monsieur Nisard pursued his reformist mission, first through a number of articles published in* La Revue des Deux Mondes, *and second through his* History of French Literature, *the first volume of which appeared in 1844. Written in a style both inflated and empty, these historical and critical studies incessantly reiterate the grand theory that Monsieur Nisard made the cornerstone of his teaching, to wit, that the French mind has been in a state of pure decadence since the seventeenth century.*

At once a bedside table and a bedside book, the latter carefully placed atop the fourteen piled volumes comprising the former, Pierre Larousse's *Great Universal Dictionary* is my preferred reading of the moment. I don't wait for raindrops to start falling. I take it with me when I go out. It'll just have to squeeze into my pocket. On a sunlit terrace or beneath a shady willow, I sit down on the first fourteen volumes and rest the fifteenth, which is in fact the eleventh (N–O), on my knees. I open it lovingly. What pleasant reading it makes! How perfectly it allows us to take the measure of all things! How clearly we see the bottom! A transparent crystal for the eye of Pierre Larousse, such is Désiré Nisard, in spite of his bulk, and there on the terrace or beneath the willow I find myself dreaming of the fragility of fine china, and the chiming music it makes when it breaks—indeed, is it not a pity to ladle potatoes onto a plate that is potentially a xylophone or a harp? Has anyone ever seen a harpsichordist eating from his harpsichord? Not merely ugly and base, such a thing would also be highly impractical. No, I find the purely alimentary usage of plates very difficult to defend. From all this, I conclude first and foremost that Nisard, once demolished, would no doubt sing less off-key—the tinkle of bone against bone signals the start of the festivities for the dancing masses. Not an hour goes by that I don't find another good reason to go on fighting the good fight.

BRIANÇON (AP) – *A motorist was sentenced Wednesday by the criminal court of Briançon (Hautes-Alpes) to five years in prison for aggravated involuntary manslaughter, and ordered to surrender his driver's license for at least seven years.*

Last June 13, at Rosans (Hautes-Alpes), traveling at an estimated 65 to 75 miles per hour, Désiré Nisard's car struck a Renault Clio that was stopped at an intersection; the violence of the collision projected the Clio for a distance of nearly 100 feet. Jeanne Sauvageot, 36, died instantly. She was pregnant with her sixth child.

The motorist had spent much of the evening in a bar and a disco-theque. His blood alcohol content was measured at .082. Traces of cannabis resin were also detected. He was driving without insurance in a car that had not undergone the mandatory inspection.

Attempting to flee the scene of the accident, Désiré Nisard struck a tree and ended up in a ditch. On their arrival, the police found him asleep.

At no point in the trial did he show any sign of remorse.

Seeking damages of 60,000 euros, the victim's family has filed a civil suit, to be heard in September.

It's high time we levied punitive sanctions against Nisard, and I mean draconian. Confiscation of his assets—ill-gotten, no one will be surprised to learn—will limit his options and opportunities. He will for instance be forced to give up on acquiring the atom bomb. Good-bye to the easy life for him, kneeling secretaries, lackeys on every floor. As for his cherished dream of controlling the short-term market, he'll have to bid it farewell in every language on earth. Obviously, the ideal would be to ruin him outright, and even reduce him to beggary! Nisard below the poverty line, there's a thought to delight every pure heart. Nisard huddled in a door-way, wrapped in grimy rags, dying of hunger and cold, what a beautiful, naïve image! My box of colored pencils lies open before me. Nisard's gaping shoe reveals his swollen foot, blue and violet, and now I've become the painter of ulcers most eagerly courted by publishers of medical encyclopedias. I have three shades of red at my disposal, I can tinker with the color scheme to my heart's content. It costs nothing, changes nothing, but I find it relaxing. Still, it's imperative that I not lose my anger. Brave hearts must not allow themselves to be lulled by illusions: they lose all their fight. They drift off to sleep. Nisard has a secret account in every bank that doesn't look at its customers too closely (and have you ever seen a pair of eyes beneath a bank's pretentious pediment?); no doubt he has a treasure buried beneath most of the trees in our forests as well. He will have bought our houses out from under us before we can dispossess him of a single sou. We know his ways all too well. He's a vile, viscous octopus, a bandit.

"This little literary quarrel of yours is turning a tad vicious, don't you think?"

"Aren't you getting a bit bored with playing the moderator, Métilde?"

"Oh, I most certainly am! So very bored!"

She raises her hard little fist, and then pow! right in Nisard's nose.

How I love her!

I'm trying to make up my mind. On the one hand there's the Conibear trap, an ingenious device, exquisitely sensitive, designed to kill the animal by breaking its back or neck in one clean snap, although in reality it more often survives, its body broken, for many agonizing hours, days, nights. And then, on the other, the Leghold trap, a pair of steel jaws fitted with a powerful spring and affixed to a base whose center is an articulated platform that gives way under the animal's weight, acting as a trigger: the jaws snap violently shut around the surprised creature's leg, its only hope of escape an excruciating self-mutilation; more likely, it will perish after hours of fruitless struggle and horrific suffering. But why this hesitation? Clearly, the answer would be to set out one of each, Conibear and Leghold both, on the footpaths and lanes Nisard frequents. Piano-wire snares have been known to slice their prey into two segments, assuming no bone stands in the way. We'll put some of those out as well. But did I breathe one word of foregoing the branch-and-leaf-covered hole with the sharpened stick at the bottom? Let's get digging!

(Word has it that black marketeers trafficking in surplus Red Army weaponry are offering land mines for purchase. Name your price. Write care of my publisher, envelope marked "please forward.")

"*Modern civilization has built two very fine things in Nîmes: a public promenade and a prison. No notion of human civilization can be truly complete unless it provides for the evil in men as well as the good. On the one hand a prison, and on the other, for free citizens, a promenade: here, then, is a complete notion of civilization.*" Thus does Nisard see the world, and such are the plans for the public welfare incubating in his beneficent heart. Let there be no doubt, he'll throw himself into this project with every ounce of strength he has in him. For his tribute to civilization and its undertakings in Nîmes is tinged with implicit reproaches and regrets—why, for example, did they not build the promenade directly in front of the prison? So elegantly simple, so utterly self-evident! The spirit of civilization would be still more powerfully affirmed: strolling past the sinister stronghold, the good people of Nîmes delight all the more in their innocence, or at least their impunity; meanwhile, behind the walls, the prisoners expiate their crimes—or, in some cases, their misfortunes, their unshakable jinx—all the more tormented by the loss of their freedom in that through the bars they can see Désiré Nisard trotting along from morning to evening, one hand clutching a cone of hot chestnuts or ice cream, depending on the season, and on his arm, one evening a week, whatever the weather, a voluptuous, hired female companion. Thus does he seek to punish vice and reward virtue, offering each up to the other for the edification of all. For Nisard is the sort of philosopher who relies on carefully chosen comparisons to counteract the relativity of things: his appetite wouldn't be so voracious if so many hungry men were not covetously eyeing his share.

Désiré's Pen-Case

1) If, at the end of this first feather quill, you were hoping to find Nisard's pulsating body, what a letdown: a stuffed stiff!

2) This one scrapes over the paper like chalk on a chalkboard, and indeed, toothaches and tedious lessons follow.

3) The third left behind a long string of hackneyed ideas, but there's a great difference between the parrot's colorful verbiage

and the mechanical repetition produced by this quill in its mono-chrome voice.

4) Yet another poultry feather that will never know what it means to fly, or to write.

5) The fifth is coarse and gray. So Nisard—but who would be surprised to hear it?—wrote with rat feathers as well!

6) From the sixth flowed still more regrets and sad remem-brances—the egg itself a sarcophagus.

7) The seventh quill, twisted, deformed, almost completely stripped of its barbs and barbules, was Nisard's pen of choice for his one-sided amorous correspondence with a peahen.

8) Well-chewed is this one, so difficult is the art of writing, and so persistent the taste of turkey.

9) The ninth plume belonged to the Cheyenne tracker who led Custer to Black Kettle's camp near the Washita River, where more than a hundred women and children were slaughtered. My ques-tion: what's it doing here?

10) Allergic to the swallow's plumes, Nisard produced with this one nothing more than a bitter, grating little cough.

11) The eleventh's nib is red with dried blood, as if Nisard used his own veins as his inkwell. But no: rather, between each word, he stuck it back into the body of the unfortunate chicken.

12 and 13) The twelfth and thirteenth were never used—only a decapitated cobra is as loveable.

14) The fourteenth is the down with which a sniveling Nisard scratched at his contemporaries.

15) The fifteenth is crushed and cracked: another angel fallen from on high.

16) The sixteenth has a bend in the middle, and points off at a curious angle. This is the finest of the bunch: it turned on Nisard.

17) Another clutch of stiff, prickly quills, which explains why none are left around the vulture's neck.

18) If, at the other end of the eighteenth, you were expecting to find a nice fat goose or a tender young pigeon, what a letdown: only that same chicken-livered buzzard, yet again.

19) The nineteenth is not actually a quill at all, but the grousing, chattering beak of a magpie.

20) And the twentieth is a coelacanth scale: never did any plume fly so low as between Nisard's fingers.

Such is the quill-case of that old feather-duster Nisard, the source of all dust: the birds' tiny coffin.

Perhaps, all along, the feathered arrow served no other purpose than to keep plumes out of Nisard's clutches? Glorious archers, firing toward the heavens or the horizon to rid the world of that terrible threat, I hereby offer you my homage, I hereby offer you my thanks. You did all you could. You alone, perhaps, merit no rebuke. Whistling merrily, your arrows clove the air, carrying their feathers far from Nisard, disappearing into the heavens or beyond the horizon, never to fall or return, and every vanished arrow meant four feathers that Nisard would never dip into an inkwell, I don't know if you grasp what that means. Four feathers that Nisard would never dip into an inkwell! I'm proud of each and every one of my sentences. I would like my reader to be so fortunate or so good as to give each one equal consideration, to meditate on them all, to devote to each a day and a night, to retreat to a mountain grotto first with one sentence and then with another, and return to the valley only after having fully extracted their sense, but I know that this cannot be, alas, that my reader sometimes lets himself be distracted by the trivial occupations and obligations of his own existence, that he has various inexplicable tasks to attend to outside my book, but I think I may justifiably ask that he linger a bit over that one sentence, at least—and really, what matter if this means foregoing the dubious pleasures of his holidays or his senseless passion for two ocular globes and a mouthful of teeth—for I have written nothing more joyous than that, that poem of the Golden Age: every arrow that vanished meant four feathers that Nisard would never dip into an inkwell. I will make my peace with my insufferable contemporaries only when they once more, en masse, take up the invigorating and hygienic practice that is archery.

And what about birds, come to think of it? What purpose do birds serve? Why birds, if not to waft feathers far from Nisard's reach? And suddenly I find myself gripped by an infinite tenderness for birds, for their individual exertions as they vigorously race away from Nisard, for their mass migrations, in limitless throngs, away from Nisard. Fragile bodies, tiny lungs, stout hearts, setting off across the Atlantic with their precious cargo of feathers: Nisard stands on the shore, stamping his feet and shaking his fist at the heavens—he'll never write again. Struggling against the wind and its insatiable appetite for destruction, the wind that would laugh to see those plumes fall straight back into Nisard's hands, the bird valiantly strives to put all possible distance between the former and the latter, forsaking its wool-carpeted nest and the cherry tree that fed and sustained it: now it's in Africa, a place of curious customs—Nisard will never come looking for it there. And should it lack the strength to propel itself to those distant climes, the bird will take all possible measures to make itself nonetheless inaccessible. It flees at the slightest sound: that could be Nisard coming. It perches on the slender branches of tall trees, where Nisard will never venture, alas (he might fall and break his neck), or atop flexible pines (whose summit bends to the ground and then suddenly snaps back, catapulting Nisard out of sight). It nests between two stones, in a hollow tree trunk, behind a curtain of ivy, silent and unseen: its feathers remain out of Nisard's reach. You were perhaps thinking that the bird feels some fondness for this vertiginous existence, that it needs ninety feet of empty air underneath it to feel light and carefree? Don't you find its arguments against the law of gravity a bit thin? With boundless energy, it contests the obvious fact of the fall, and maintains its position in defiance of common sense, at the price of endless acrobatics—and all that for its own delight, to satisfy its own desire, is that seriously what you think? The bird has chosen to give unstintingly of itself; a mere minuscule black or white dot in the sky, the bird, to the best of its ability and until the fated moment of its death, keeps feathers out of Nisard's grasp.

No doubt the most surprising thing in a book without Nisard would be the light. I'm convinced of it: habituated as he is to a certain textual obscurity born of the shadow cast by Nisard, the reader would first of all be amazed by all the light. No longer would Désiré Nisard be blocking its source. The reader would next delight in the quality of the silence that precedes and follows every truly meaningful utterance, a silence currently disturbed by Nisard's endless carping—is he not even now grumbling and fidgeting petulantly in his chair? There is however one sound emanating from him, and one sound only, that our ear would be curious to hear: what manner of reverberation would be produced by the insect-demolishing slap to his cheek? In the book without Nisard, no more gasping for fresh air, no more nostrils pinched shut. To be sure, it's hard to believe that the sea breeze is still blowing when the grounded sperm whale lies rotting on the shore, the atmosphere choked with its effluvia; cart off that putrid flesh, however, and the reader will breathe a great deal easier. As will the non-reader too, in the world without Nisard.

But we're not there yet, alas, and the struggle for his eradication still has far to go. In the fall, vulnerable leaves are dotted with winter eggs (oospores) that can withstand the most frigid temperatures (up to ten degrees below zero); these germinate in the spring, once the average temperature exceeds fifty-two degrees, producing macroconidia, which, under the effect of rainwater or dew, release zoospores. These first stages of the parasite's development soon lead to primary infections: by way of the stomata—microscopic pores in the tissue, through which gases are exchanged—the zoospores penetrate the underside of the leaves, the tendrils, and the new shoots. Once inside the host tissue, the fungus proliferates. In damp, mild weather it forms a cottony down on the bunch stems or the underside of the leaves, producing new sporangia that will in turn release zoospores, soon spread by rainfall, causing still more infections. Affected leaves are first marked by yellowish discolorations; once necrosis sets in, they dry out and fall. The young shoots and the clusters wither, shrivel, wrinkle, and die. Coated with a whitish layer of spores, the fruits lose their turgidity and finally fall from the stem. Various strategies have been devised to counter this process, some of them reputedly successful, though never entirely so, and besides, to be frank, the idea of eliminating Nisard by means of a fungicide seems to me an example of the most breathtaking naïveté.

Sometimes, can you hear it, a sob chokes my voice, it's too much to take, it's unbearable. I can stand no more. Tears raining down, I throw myself on my bed. Then I get up again, close the shutters, the curtains, I need darkness, total darkness, darkness without Nisard. There, that's better. What a relief! But it takes only one ray of moonlight, one passing torch or headlight beam, even one single firefly, to reveal his furtive presence, or at least the trace of his passage, of his influence or effect on the briefly illuminated scene around me. I stuff rags between the slats of the shutters, I push a rolled-up rug under the door. I seal myself away. In the darkness, I recover some semblance of serenity. All is tranquility—a deceptive tranquility, in which weapons are readied and treacheries plotted. Can I really have forgotten that all darkness emanates from Nisard?

The hour of nightmares has sounded, the time of obsessive fears and dark forebodings. Métilde is sleeping beside me. I touch her with my foot or fingertips. I'm so afraid of finding her stiff and cold, I have to make certain she's still alive: and yes, somehow she's still soldiering on, weathering the storm, how does she do it? After all, she can't take herself in her own arms. And yet I know from experience that her embrace offers the only comfort, the sole consolation in this world wholly subjugated to Nisard's dominion. But all at once I pull away. I consider Métilde warily. I thought I glimpsed Nisard's grimace deforming her revered features. I saw a great, shifty eye rolling under her brow. How square, suddenly, are her fingers, how thick her tongue! I don't recognize those wizened thighs, covered with short brown hairs, and what is that flabby belly, still regularly pummeled by my erect member, similar in every way to a baby's arm (for the child to be born first shows itself between its father's legs, vigorously raising its fist)—what is this monstrous coupling in which I find myself . . . against my will, kicking and screaming . . . taking part? Brutally I shove Nisard away, horrified, revolted, and a mortified Métilde runs off to lock herself in the bathroom.

At such times I find myself without friends. Nor can liquor console me. There's only Larousse, who always knows what to say: *For*

Monsieur Nisard, the century of Louis XIV is not only the literary ideal, but also the political and social ideal; the language of Boileau is the model to be imitated, and the French have written only in patois ever since; it was to this language, along with the exquisite politesse that marked that era's social customs, that France owed its supremacy in Europe. Before Malherbe and after Massillon, there is nothing in literature worthy of our attention, and our social customs have been perverted along with our language. Here, once again, is Désiré Nisard depicted dead to rights, an old crab who thinks he's laying eggs when he is in fact merely drooling, who takes every bubble of saliva or bile on his shirt front for a new idea waiting to hatch. Just as the fob watch can only run slow today, no matter how masterful the jeweler who set it, Nisard's opinions evoke an obsolete order that even the worthies of *Hunting, Fishing, Nature, and Tradition* will no longer deem so desirable when they find themselves ordered to trade in their gleaming rifles for pikes and their carbon-fiber fishing rods for bone harpoons, in accordance with the fourth article of their credo. And here I must speak directly to my reader, not without some reluctance, for I know how often he is solicited, probed, questioned, hectored, and no doubt he would sometimes prefer to be left in peace, at least when he's reading, but I only have three questions to ask you, and then you can be on your way: What is the state of your relationship with Massillon? When did you last open his collection of homilies and funerary orations? Would you be pleased to receive his *Lenten Sermons* for your next birthday?

NANTES (AFP) – *Police sources report that a 14-year-old Nantes schoolboy was seriously wounded Wednesday, shortly after 7 A.M., as he got off the bus he was riding to school.*

Stabbed three times in the abdomen, the adolescent was hospitalized in Nantes (Loire-Atlantique) in very serious condition. As of late Wednesday morning, his doctors described his prognosis as uncertain.

Witnesses report that the youth had had a violent disagreement with an unknown middle-aged man on the 64 bus between the Nantes suburb of Saint-Herblain, where the victim lives, and the Cours Guisteau in central Nantes. Seeing the teen disembark at that stop, the older man followed, attacking him as soon as he was off the bus.

Investigators are working to determine the aggressor's identity.

Who holds me back just when I was about to give in to the music, who kicks me behind the knees to force me down onto the narrow bench against the wall? Whose is the hand that smacks me on the nape to make me bow my head before the master? Who wants to see me ashamed, humiliated, fearful in every situation, and considers timidity a good boy's greatest virtue? Who makes me mute and obtuse around girls? Who dreams of a world peopled by hunchbacked, blushing children? Who spreads cruel rumors to feed my self-loathing? Who pours syrupy nostalgia over every embittered evocation of childhood? Who smears my shoe soles with that glue? Who rubs my head in my own filth and then claims to see no difference between me and it? Who raises his voice when

I can't come up with the right words? Who uses the yardstick only to measure how small I am? Who, nonetheless, wants to make of me a warrior, a brute, a domestic tyrant?

You'd like to buy a fedora to class up your look, a sombrero to brush up your Spanish, a riding helmet to spur your horse over the plains, a bowler to revive vaudeville, a cap to grow younger, a ski-mask to redistribute the wealth, a cloche to let the ladies have their say, a crown to be obeyed, a boater to sport on your country outings, a top hat to marry Métilde, sorry, Nisard Haberdashers sells nothing but nightcaps.

And our only entertainment would be the spectacle he offers us, and the exhaustive account of his wild, madcap life: "*The steamboat continued on to Arles, and left me alone on the dock with several barrels of beer from Lyon.*"

We sit in the stands—not the stands of a bullring, alas—and look on as Nisard lives his life. We would gladly have slept a bit longer, but he's an early riser. Clad only in long johns and an undershirt of a whiteness as dubious as the immaculate conception, he spends several minutes with his chamberpot, his jug and basin, amid a tinkling and clanking of porcelain. Next he dresses: same outfit as ever, no doubt once black, now gone green in places with wear, or gone yellow, there are even glints of rainbow here and there. A cravat, long and wide enough to serve as precisely what its appearance reveals it to be: handkerchief, bib, and wipe. There is reason to fear that the two pointed hobnail shoes he finally pulls on are in fact, despite their continuous, privileged proximity, the most ill-placed to give him a good swift kick in the ass. Mere moments into this wretched performance, the audience's interest flags. And when Nisard requests a pot of weak tea and some marmalade from his servant, the floorboards shudder under the jolt of a mass nodding-off. For his morning constitutional, Nisard pulls on a frock coat like no one has made for a hundred and fifty years. Strolling the boulevards, he vaguely tries out a few twirls of his walking stick, but if life really must inflict this sort of display on us, we'd vastly prefer a parade of bare majorette thighs, thank you very much. Then Nisard goes off to legislate or profess, whichever is required by his post of the moment, and our snores echo those of his students or peers: nineteenth-century man did not laugh at exactly the same jokes as we, he was moved by a different sort of beauty, but if you cut him he did indeed bleed, and when Nisard began blathering from his rostrum he did indeed immediately commence sawing wood. Now the hour of his noontime meal has come. Nisard stuffs his face with roast beef and sautéed potatoes or stew. Everything he swallows we will vomit up. The afternoon has begun, and here's where things turn truly ugly, for Nisard is entering his study. He sits down at his desk. Alas, his intentions are no longer in doubt. Oh, for the love of God! He's going to write!

Oh, for the love of God! His trousers are down around his ankles, denuding his bony legs, bluish-white, yellowish-white, and hairy. Now comes a series of little groans and digestive gurgles. His jaws clench. The blood rises to his face. His eyes are moist. For the first time, I see a tear trickle down his cheek.

I'm considering stabbing him in the back.

Not very honorable, but I'm seriously considering stabbing him in the back, just to be sure. I don't want to blow my chance. He might try to fend me off, maybe wound me in the struggle. No thanks. In any case, as of now I consider my every act to be committed in self-defense. Nisard's a prowler. He's everywhere. I can't let down my guard, not even when his back is exposed; he can rear up like an ill-tempered horse, in addition to which his front half might be anywhere at all: no way to be entirely sure, as I plunge my long, razor-sharp knife between his ribs, just above the waist, so that my blade will skewer the rest of him too. Moreover, success would mean foregoing the pleasure of watching the life drain from his face—and what a sight that would be, the pallor of death on Nisard's cheeks, wondrous as a snowfall in Mali, an unhoped-for delight for the masses, I'd be sorry to miss it. And sorry too, understandably I think, that he'd have no idea who was dealing the fatal blow: I have my pride, my amour-propre, and when I perform such a feat, I like to have witnesses. I might even have offered him one final smile . . . But these considerations carry little weight next to what is, after all, my life's goal: Nisard's elimination. And that end justifies any means, everything is on the table: stabbing Nisard in the back seems to me an excellent idea.

Or in his sleep?

Another excellent idea. Under cover of darkness, I squeeze through a rooftop window and drop into his digs. After first scaling his building's façade, of course—a lizard having difficulty making the same ascent asked me my secret: I hate Nisard, I replied. Now I'm in. I feel my way through the unlit interior, cluttered with sharp-cornered furniture and hideous gewgaws (I can tell), smelling of stale air, cold tobacco, and aging bachelor—a musky smell, they call it, but in this case that scarcely seems fair to the noble musk-ox, whose perfume perhaps only a boxer's nose can fully appreciate. No, Nisard's scent is a sour little pall of ill-digested garlic and ill-maintained linens. It makes your heart and your stomach cling together for dear life in your throat. I fumble for a ship's railing to lean over and return all those fish-heads to the sea. It is then that I stumble onto the old man's bedroom. He's sprawled out on his back. So it's settled: I won't be stabbing him from behind. Like many a churchman's, Nisard's graceless body is not as thin as it looks—was he ever sincere about anything? For his hitched-up nightshirt reveals two spindly legs, comically (why, then, these tears in my eyes?) fitted to a chubby body, comfited in its own fat. What beautiful words could such a vision possibly inspire in me, it's ugly, it's sad, it's repellent: only human flesh can endure such deformations, only human flesh can expand in every direction and every manner like this, as if the skeleton counted for nothing—never will we see the frog, the ass, or the butterfly in any form but their own, they hold to it proudly, even late in old age or in the throes of some illness, the ass remains a statue of an ass, the frog a figurine of a frog, the butterfly a replica of a butterfly, but what does Nisard resemble? I waver. I can no sooner imagine planting a knife than a fork in that mountain of butter, I could never bear the feel of it. What a horrific sight! That smug belly seems to swell with each intake of breath. I retreat to a corner in terror. Abandoned, my knife gleams on the bedside rug. Slowly I creep toward the door, back pressed to the wall. The stairway. The street. Once again, I take to my heels and flee.

My shoelaces seem to be forever coming undone—it's the blades of grass I keep tying up, two by two: I love the fog, where every confusion can be justified. The invisible cow swinging its tail in a field might just as well be me feather-dusting my tables and shelves, for weeks I'd been putting off tackling that little chore, now it's done. But most of all I love the fog because it brings with it the disappearance of Nisard's world: a miracle worth every divine apparition put together. And so we have to invent. I seize the moment to change my identity. I am the spider in that immense web. Anything that gets caught up in it is mine. Sometimes, of course, I run into something hard or pointed, something that seems solid, that resists—thus does the amputee go on feeling his phantom limb: my nerves retain their memory of the obliterated world. These unpleasant sensations would pass, if only the fog would keep up . . . *ROAAAH* . . . You heard that roar, same as me. Where are we? Geography is an outmoded notion. As is chronology: we wander aimlessly through the ages, our own left far behind . . . *'SDEATH!* . . . Did you hear that?

Let no one misunderstand, I too am very fond of a certain seventeenth-century literature. Undeniably, there are some fine things to be found there. For example, Nisard, take a listen to this:

> *I'll allow thee to choose the means of thy demise:*
> *With one blow of my fist I might thee pulverize,*
> *Thrust thee to the earth's core where none will hear your cries,*
> *Or with ten backhand slices cut thee down to size,*
> *Or else launch thee so far into the azure skies*
> *That celestial fires will thee carbonize.*
> *Make thy choice, then, and quickly, and say thy good-byes.*

Yes, I can like Corneille, when he's giving it his all, even if literature has since evolved, perhaps progressed, even if today I would instead write:

> I will grant you a death full of bliss and delight:
> I'll burst you like a wineskin with one gentle bite
> And dive deep into you like an otter in flight,
> Drape myself in your flesh, a loving transvestite,

Drink your semen and blood with lustful appetite—
And the nocturnal vampire, erstwhile stalactite,
Finding you cold and drained will trudge into the night.

The world has changed, and literature along with it—from Corneille to your humble servant (my letter of resignation is on your desk), the progress is patent. We've long since left the realm of comic illusions. The threats I make here will have real consequences. Nisard will never get back on his feet. I'm taking bets. After this book, he'll never be mentioned again. At best, his name will become a synonym for "buffoon." That's how I intend to revive him (post-execution).

There would thus be a great deal to say, too, about Désiré Nisard's physical person, and more than enough to ridicule, but on principle I am loath to mock the unsightlinesses that afflict my fellow men (who must have fallen out of the tree while they were descending from the apes), and besides I am fully aware that the muttonchop whiskers that obscure half his face, on the one hand, corresponded to the style of the time, which, however ridiculous, was nonetheless widespread, and on the other, obscured half his face, for which we should be deeply thankful, as always when our poor world is spared some great tribulation. Nevertheless, his nose still emerges from that brushy tangle of hair, and so we must regret that the style of the time did not encourage the sporting of full-coverage mustaches, or protruding beards meant to be braided to the bangs on the forehead, or perhaps eyebrows in curtain form.

Thus, to the chagrin of man and the blighting of the landscapes in which it turned up, there was Nisard's inept face, his dismaying visage sometimes appeared at windows, a sad, sad apparition.

DIVERSE APPARITIONS OF NISARD

You were, for example, a little girl, merrily skipping up the Boulevard des Capucines; along the way, you could well have run into Nisard. The risk was very real. A little later, the same girl might be spied once again, now anguished, hunched, and haggard, hobbling down the Rue des Filles-du-Calvaire.

There was a perfectly round lake, its calm waters sparkling in the rays of the loving sun. Roes and does came there to drink, as did does and roes. The water was home to magnificent carps—orange, violet, golden, inedible—left in peace by the local anglers, and to frogs, naked as love and fresh water. Then Nisard came along to admire his reflection.

An eager throng pouring into the theater, taking their seats with bated breath. Electricity in the air, joyous anticipation. Everyone is elegantly attired. The evening promises to be a delight. The lights go down. And then, on the empty stage, appears Nisard.

Those mountains are nothing other than a great pile of fallen rocks, but where from, and how? Only one explanation: there were once many more moons in the firmament, but then their rays encountered Nisard; rather than illuminate his silhouette and cast his shadow, they must have chosen to jump ship. In vain, every night, do we drop the remaining one into the trash can by our front door, hoping to be done once and for all with Nisard's nocturnal apparitions: night falls, and there it is shining on him anew, like a spotlight.

The celebrations were at their peak. The music stretched out its arms, eager to enfold us. We danced. Gay, smiling faces on all sides. So rarely do we experience the simple joy of being together, without epidemics, without allergies. For once we felt happy and serene in the human horde. Then Nisard made his entrance, hideous to see, repellent, and the crowd split in two as he passed. The next day, the two camps were at war.

Nisard blows on his hot milk, and now he has a cupful of butter for his toast. He dips his finger in the wine, and now he has a glassful of vinaigrette for his leek.

I'm not proud to say it, having previously announced my complete lack of interest, but I've restarted my search for *A Milkmaid Succumbs*. Nothing has come of my inquiries, and no new leads have cropped up. I write off to libraries, blindly, hoping for a miracle. Oh, so it would be a miracle, would it? protests Métilde, who has taken up arms in my struggle, and often proves even fiercer than I toward Nisard, her arguments all the more cutting in that she's given up biting her nails forever. A miracle, eh? Getting your hands on that smutty bagatelle, that would be a miracle, would it? All right, all right, Métilde, you're right, I retract that word. But just think: what a windfall, if we could get hold of that wretched thing! Something for us to laugh over, and yet another performance by that sorry clown, one of his finest, I've no doubt. Métilde nods, but something seems to be troubling her. The Nisard that we know, she finally says, is a loathsome character, no goose's beak quacks louder than that puckered ass, his snoot cries out for the fist like a mare's odoriferous vulva for the stallion's formidable member, his judgment is infallibly as ill-advised as a chortle of condolence. The cretin has never ceased to demonstrate his inability to appreciate a book at its true worth, and that's precisely what worries me: if he thought this one deserved to be wiped from the face of the earth, perhaps it was brilliant, the wondrous outpouring of a Nisard still pure, the magnificent blaze of a superior mind flaming out, a Nisard with no tomorrow, then, a brother to Rimbaud or Ducasse, another genius gone too soon, a beautiful soul, soaring, aglow, soon to be only a gray, spiteful ghost once the fire's died away.

Well, in that case, Métilde, we'll shame him: throw his masterpiece in his teeth, wave it back and forth in his face, caress it, recite it: See what you once were, Nisard, and see what you have become! No point hitting the heights if it's only to tumble all the faster into the cesspool. But, my dear, this is an exceedingly remote possibility we're talking about. Let me remind you, after all, that this *Season in Hell* bears the title *A Milkmaid Succumbs*.

symptoms
Progressive loss of feeling and motor function. The affected area is generally quite small at first, perhaps nothing more than one segment of a limb (a toe, for example); it loses its warmth and gradually darkens; finally necrosis sets in. The damage spreads spontaneously to nearby tissues. There follows a dramatic rise in the victim's temperature, accompanied by intense pain and prostration.

treatment
Amputation.

I discover the ravages wrought by Nisard in myself. Would I be so weary of all things if I didn't detect Nisard's touch in their workings? He orders this world in his cramped, narrow skull, and now beauty itself is befouled by the background against which its pure forms must appear, or rather the viscous morass into which it will inevitably be plunged. Water and fire are stuffed into the same drawer: we'll have to make do with a cloud of steam when we need either one. Such is Nisard's notion of order. The lioness lies down by man's bedside, spread-eagled, accorded less respect than his comforter. No music to be heard but in church. The whip was rising heavenward just now, but it will be back, best wait where you are, it'll be down before you know it. At first light of day, we'll find the farmer in the field and the sailor at sea: two brothers who will never meet. On the other hand, their children are enrolled together at Désiré Nisard Elementary. Everything is in its place, and yet lovers spend years seeking each other out before—purely by chance—they finally meet.

PARIS (AFP) – *In a Tuesday, August 3 interview on RTL Radio, Désiré Nisard reaffirmed his position that France's minimum wage is overly generous, adding that nothing had been decided concerning the plan for periodic increases and that his organization intends to pressure the government to push back the dates. He also called once again for a relaxation of the law that established the 35-hour workweek.*

Any increase in management's mandatory pension payments for low-earning workers would have "a truly traumatic effect on French entrepreneurship," according to Désiré Nisard.

Finally, he stated that the 2005 budget's elimination of "only 8,000 government jobs out of 2.6 million" shows that "we still have a long way to go."

It is too often forgotten that in 1852—the very year in which Nisard offered the Second Empire the unwavering support of his convictions and his pen, too long enjoyed solely by Republicans and Monarchists—Léonard Nodot, founder and director of the city of Dijon's Museum of Natural History, took delivery of some twenty wooden crates shipped from the distant land of Uruguay. Thus, as Désiré Nisard was piling up the tedious pages of his *History of French Literature*, Nodot pried off the wooden lids one by one, discovering in the straw the disassembled skeleton and disembodied scales of a strange fossil creature. It cost him four sleepless months of painstaking labor to reconstruct the animal. The God of Genesis started from scratch, things were easy back then, plenty of room for whimsy, extravagance, improvisation, whereas Léonard had to rely on lucidity, patience, and logic to put his grotesque monster back on its feet. Whose job is it to pick up the pieces? Léonard's. And why him? Nobody knows. Finally the glyptodont was reconstituted and set upright, solidly poised on its four feet with the aid of a discreet armature of wood and iron. It had breathed its last on a bed of grass two million years before, emitting a brief, guttural cry with no name (man having only much later assigned the bray, the squeal, the growl, and the whinny, in his peremptory little falsetto). One last convulsion shook the giant beast's body, and its noble head lolled to one side. Big as my fists, its eyes finally closed, and soon the tigers, the vultures, the cloudbursts set about dismantling it. And now, as Nisard was idly compiling Latin authors, Léonard Nodot had revived it, or perhaps invented it with the scales of eight hundred tortoises, a horse's head, and four rhinoceros feet. Its massive tail is made up of six articulated segments, studded with bony spikes. What a weapon! I know what head I'd smash with that mace!

Whenever I have a minute to myself, I run straight to Dijon's Museum of Natural History, fast as my legs will take me. Ferrari lags far behind, puffing and red. I race through the streets, my body dissolving into a mere speeding blur. On arriving, I reassemble myself, yes, it's me. I'm here. This is the place. I push open the glass door and enter the museum's cool, slightly musty dimness. A chance to catch my breath at last. Nonetheless, I stride briskly past the exhibits in the first drab, dusty rooms, so hemmed in by display cases as to evoke some endless corridor in a boarding school or barracks, packed with everything one has a right to dread in a provincial natural history museum: the *entire* genealogy of Jurassic ammonites, a sample of *every* sort of sedimentary rock to be found in Burgundy (rhyolite, red granite, white granite, two-mica granite, albitophyre, orthophyre, pegmanite with large quartz crystals and tourmaline, barytine, fluorine), a stuffed inventory of local fauna (heron, marsh warbler, spotted crake, garden dormouse, roe deer, wild boar, incredulous emaciated hedgehog, fox, pike), the inevitable jars of salamander marmalade and axolotl jam, a yellow-bellied toad adrift since 1845 in a deep alcoholic stupor, an asp refracted in formaldehyde: a sword in the water. Now it's behind me.

One broad glazed cabinet still stands in my way. *The evolution of primates, and particularly of hominids, can be compared to a vast fireworks display. Is there more to come? We have no way of knowing,* reads the legend. And I am forthwith invited to admire the show. Multitudinous showers of sparks indeed, white, yellow, and pink: shards of skulls or femurs rain down, orangutan, pithecanthropus, robust and gracile australopithecus (a comical couple, even then), Neanderthal, Tautavel man, and finally, in one last bouquet of long and short bones, the miraculously complete skeleton of the pyrotechnician himself, *sapiens sapiens*. This is simply a thing to be got through. It's the price you must pay for a tête-à-tête with Léonard Nodot's glyptodont, in whose scaly dome the dreams of Renaissance architects had already come true. Look at Florence's Duomo: you will find neither the majesty nor the sensuous curve of that shell. The celestial vault does not cover the world so perfectly. And oh, the acoustics . . .

A glance to the right, a glance to the left. The coast is clear. Nimbly I scale the glass panel protecting the animal. I duck under the impeccable cupola. I wouldn't be shocked to find frescoes by Giotto on the walls, incense in the air. It's cool, but not cold. The dim light is welcoming, prehistoric. I could settle in here for good, in this bubble, this silence, why not? But on second thought, no: I remember why I'm here. I clear my throat. And, with all the might of my fully inflated lungs, I let loose: NISARD! I HATE YOU! The museum windows rattle. Outside, the tall plane trees bend low over the lawn. I hurry out of my shell. I'm not particularly proud of myself. Did the glyptodont so long hold its tongue only to end up giving vent to that piteous bawl? Is this, then, the Eureka of its long solitary meditation? Remorse washes over me. Cheeks burning, I leave the museum.

But I know I'll be back, back to cry out again, there's no resisting it. It's the same thing every time. I vow to stop inflicting this shame on myself, and yet back I go. For a few days I hold off, a few weeks, I've never yet managed more than a month. Then I start cheating on my resolutions. I spend my nights pulling stars from the sky, on the pretext of donating them to Léonard Nodot's collection. Morning comes, and I can't very well not hand them over. And slowly I drift toward the large room at the back, soon I'm in it, I'm under the glyptodont, and immediately my song rises into the airs. NISARD! I HATE YOU!, and the echo whirls under the scaly vault, rebounds endlessly against the walls of that drum—thus amplified, it erupts from my glyptodont's bony mouth: wherever you are, you will hear it.

Someday I will also intone into that magical trumpet the confidences proffered by Monsieur Larousse: *Désiré Nisard displays no curiosity, nor indeed any of the historian's requisite qualities. How does he choose those illustrious names that supplant all the rest? Why these rather than others? He takes care not to explain; he merely affirms that France recognizes itself in Racine and begins to no longer recognize itself in Jean-Jacques Rousseau. Beneath their grandiose veneer, these are the narrowest theories that can be applied to the literary study of a nation, and Monsieur Nisard would reiterate just such inanities without surcease in his every academic discourse to come.*

Léonard Nodot and Pierre Larousse: so Nisard had at least two contemporaries engaged in vast and ambitious endeavors. In 1837, the former offers the publisher Douillier his *Report to Monsieur the Mayor of Talant on the Possibility of having an Abundant Spring at the Foot of the Hillock on which this Town is Situated*, and, while Nisard publishes without letup and without care, as one might hurl brickbats, Léonard Nodot will subsequently entrust to print only brief mineralogical descriptions in the interest of science, believing he has nothing to add to the content of that *Report*, in which we can see his concern for the well-being of his fellow citizens and his conviction that the Roman Empire's system of water distribution was no longer suited to the needs of his age. As for the hydraulic engineers and well-diggers of the seventeenth century, they likely had too much on their hands with the Great Waters of Versailles to think of pouring drinks for the good people of Talant. The least we could do would be to rehabilitate Nodot as he himself did the glyptodont, carefully setting him back on his feet, forgetting not a single one of his little bones, and remaking him in all his former glory. *Restoring Nodot*, such could have been the title of this book, had I not conceived another plan, which I cherish deep in my heart, and which overrules all the rest.

But let us imagine, at least: in the mud of the cemetery, I dig. I push aside the brambles, I lift the slab covering his grave, and there in the pit lies the coffin of Léonard Nodot. I hoist it out. The worms have not wholly devoured it; it withstands the exhumation, and then the transfer, intact. Like Léonard himself opening the crates that contained the glyptodont, which is to say with a rough iron bar and a tender look, I lift the lid. He's inside. It's him. The lead mille-feuille encasing him has slowed the process of obliteration. His flesh has melted away, it's true. Not much left of the hearty drinker and merry tablemate. Nor of his clothing. One observation, nevertheless: nothing more closely resembles an electrocuted rat than the leathery crust of a shriveled shoe on a human foot's delicate ossature. The many dislocated bones of his frame will have to be screwed back together, but I think I'm up to that task. I will devotedly see it through. Let us restore Nodot. And then we'll display him in one of his glass cases as *sapiens sapiens'* most accomplished exemplar. In a box at his feet, the shame of the species, a pulverized castoff, the ashy residue of Nisard.

Jean-Marie-Napoléon-Désiré Nisard is born in Châtillon-sur-Seine on March 20, 1806, at number 4, Rue au Lait. His parents belong to the unmoneyed provincial petite-bourgeoisie. His father, Hilaire-François-Alexandre Nisard (1776–1822), is a solicitor to the civil magistrates' court of the city. His mother, Marie-Scolastique Miel (born in 1778—date and circumstances of her death under investigation), who married Hilaire on the 11th of Vendémiaire, year 12, will give him three brothers and three sisters. As a child, he is caught attempting to steal apples. He falls from the orchard wall and rises to his feet, in his own words, "hurt and humiliated." On learning of his misdeed, the orchard's owner demands reparations, and the child is made to kneel in the courtyard of his school with a necklace of apples around his neck, to Hilaire and Scolastique's profound shame. In 1832, Désiré marries the unfortunate Élisabeth Ball (1806–1890), and that same year the couple brings into the world their only child, a daughter,

Marie-Élisabeth (1832–1899), who, on July 2, 1855, will marry Édouard Romberg (1818–1899). Désiré Nisard dies in San Remo on March 25, 1888. The Nisard name dies with him. A life, then, a destiny, a biography full of dates and facts; nothing more is required, nothing else really matters.

One day, too, Nisard is delighted to find in the Ossau valley none of the corruptions too commonplace elsewhere for his liking, "*neither those horrid women, so dirty, so afflicted with goiters, almost all of them mothers before they were wives, nor those ugly, swarming children of such uncertain parentage who jump or crawl around your carriage at the entrance to every village.*" If that isn't nobility of soul and sentiment, just you try and tell me what it is. Moral abjection? Yes, no doubt one could call it that as well. You've got to show your compassion somehow, and this is Nisard's, Nisard who yearns for the extermination of those vermin, the eradication of the poor folk infesting the social body. Strange parasites, however, if I may permit myself to intervene in the debate despite the strict neutrality I've vowed to observe throughout this book, strange parasites who find no profit, neither warmth nor nourishment, in the fur of their host.

There was also the time Nisard suffered a bad bump to the elbow; there was the time Nisard broke his nose against a windowpane he'd failed to see; there was the time an embarrassing stain on Nisard's back aroused the hilarity of passersby; there was Nisard's sprained ankle and the grain of sand beneath Nisard's eyelid; Nisard's toothache; the bee-sting; Nisard slipping and falling on a patch of ice; there was the cloudburst that caught Nisard unawares; there was the time Nisard bit his tongue and the time he pinched his finger in a door; there was the mosquito in Nisard's bedroom and the fishbone caught in his throat; there was the bedbug in his bed; which is why, in spite of everything, Nisard's existence was not entirely pointless.

By hook or by crook, I forge contacts with nineteenth-century specialists. I slip into university buildings, I study the faculty directories, then watch for scholars of that era's literature or history as they exit their lecture halls. I approach them on the most tenuous pretexts, reluctant to broach too overtly the subject that preoccupies me. A certain level of intimacy is required, I believe, before such secrets can be dragged out into the open: Are you familiar with Nisard, Désiré Nisard? Have you heard of his novel *A Milkmaid Succumbs*? Would you by any chance own a copy? Do you know where I might find one? It would obviously be boorish to subject the nineteenth-century specialists I meet to the harsh glare of these questions right off the bat, and I couldn't expect them to answer me frankly without my first gaining their trust. Whence a series of refined little dinners at my expense: they eat prodigiously, and I drink in their words, to wash it all down. From hors-d'oeuvres to dessert I nod my head knowingly, an admiring smile on my lips. Sometimes I push my obsequiousness so far as to jot down one of their remarks on the tablecloth, then carefully tear it out and slip it lovingly into my wallet, as if it held the secret of life. After several weeks of this burdensome intercourse, I take the plunge and ask my first question: (*casually*) Are you familiar with Nisard, Désiré Nisard? And in fact every nineteenth-century specialist knows of Nisard, and on hearing their affirmative response, my heart beats faster, I reel, I feel an intoxicating hope being reborn in my darkened recesses. I savor that euphoria for a few days before pursuing my inquiries further: (*offhandedly*) Have you heard of his novel *A Milkmaid Succumbs*? Finding the entire edifice of their expertise menaced by this question, the nineteenth-century specialists generally play along, but I've already stopped believing them, and when I ask if they've read it themselves, they can only confess, for fear of being found out, that they've never so much as seen a copy of the thing, never held it in their hands. Abruptly I rise from the table, my chair toppling backward. This time, dinner's on them.

Dare I tell you, Métilde, I engaged in a three-month affair with a well-aged Alsatian nineteenth-century specialist, a certain Fabiola, simply because her original training as a seventeenth-century specialist had exposed her to Nisard's writings on that Golden Age, leaving her better versed in his work than her colleagues? Between two amorous encounters—as exhausting as they were unimpassioned, Métilde, please believe me—while she withdrew to the bathroom to reconstruct the mask of makeup and cream she'd left with her lingerie among the rumpled sheets, I painstakingly searched her boudoir for the sought-after volume. Fabiola wasn't slow to catch on: she adopted a mysterious air whenever I mentioned Nisard's book, to suggest that she did indeed own a copy and thus maintain her hold over me. Failing to find it on the shelves of her personal library, I concluded she'd hidden it away in some secret spot. Having become her sex slave, I was ordered to crawl like a dog on her bedroom's cold tile floor: I took advantage of the moment to peek under the furniture. I found nothing. Then she fell for a hot-blooded medievalist and sent me packing. Closing her door for the last time, she held out a copy of *The Lily of the Valley*, that's the book you were after, wasn't it? The milkmaid must have stumbled on some country lane, and that's how your pale heroine ended up in the mud at the bottom of that ditch.

Just you try telling me any such thing, answers Métilde, evidently unwilling to concede that the quest for knowledge brings with it certain joyless obligations to which the dogged seeker must simply resign himself, lest all his labors come to naught.

See what an unquenchable source of vexations this Nisard constitutes! One hundred and seventeen years after his death, he still foments discord in my household. What did I ever do to him, that he should assail me so relentlessly? And why should he find so intolerable the sweet harmony of my home? What tempests he sometimes unleashes within my four walls! Whence comes this crimson, frenzied Métilde before me? Who is this Fury lacerating my face with her nails? All these tears, all these imprecations merely because I slept with an aging nineteenth-century specialist, and perhaps also two or three of her students writing Master's theses on the birth of literary criticism or the fancifully licentious mode of the literature of the 1830s.

But don't expect me to become a specialist in the works of that parasite, for that's what he undeniably is, as a quick genealogical overview will confirm. Phylum: Platyhelminthes. Class: Cestoidea. Order: Cyclophyllidea. Family: Taeniidae. So much for his ancestry. Physically speaking, a ribbon-like form, up to thirty-five or forty feet long. Behind the head lies the growth area; here, new egg-bearing segments known as proglottids are continually produced, and shed once they mature, whereupon they are expelled in the stool, causing a very disagreeable itch. The head, known as the scolex, is anchored to the intestine by means of four suckers. The patient quickly loses weight. He suffers horrible abdominal cramps. No one wants him for a husband. More time goes by. If he doesn't die of depletion, he sometimes succeeds in ridding himself of the ignoble worm by vomiting it through his mouth.

The book without Nisard would be poetry in its purest form. Drive Nisard from your pages, you ladies and gentlemen of letters, and you'll scarcely believe that what remains could have come from your pen: pure poetry. It was simply a matter of expunging Nisard. And yet, what skill that demands! The book without Nisard will open up vast new realms for meditation and musing, of course, but the body will not be forgotten: there'll be plenty of room for its frolics. No doubt said body will at first be bewildered to find itself suddenly invited to enter a book and breathe the fresh air, as pure as on some mountaintop, some April morning, when it was expecting only stifling confinement in a hermetically sealed chamber; heretofore, whenever it ventured into a book, this body's nose always encountered the odor of Nisard, and we know how he lets himself go, for all his hygienist-censor airs. His underclothes have aged along with him. His breath is the subtle bird-call that puts cockroaches in a romantic mood. Nevertheless, the book without Nisard would strive to be something more than a manifesto for a world without Nisard: rather, a detailed plan for a world without Nisard; not just another utopia, but the promise of the world without Nisard, simultaneously expressed and kept. No landscape of the world with Nisard can give any idea of the world without Nisard, neither lake nor mountain peak nor prairie nor dune. No representation can do it justice. We stand on the threshold of that emotion, whose mere foretaste simultaneously delights us— somewhere else, in some time to come, perhaps, we'll know that joy—and torments us, for here and now, assuredly, we still have so far to go.

Dreams are born of a lethal slippage into the quicksand of sleep. Like a dying man's, the sleeper's passive brain is invaded by a rush of jumbled, incoherent images from the life he's leaving behind. Impotently he endures the bombardment: all his baggage comes flying at him. And his father's belts and his mother's wigs. Here is his first girlfriend's hand: he recognizes the ring, bought in Antibes. He knows from which garden comes that fragment of rust-colored gravel, and in what living room that belligerent dachshund is barking. Yes, this watch is indeed his watch. Here indeed is the sky he can see from his window. But what about that lion disemboweling those black and white cows? He's never spent time among lions. It took nothing more than the old claw-foot tub that served as a watering trough in his childhood village, that and the word "bloodbath," spotted the day before in the financial pages, to give rise to this carnage. Recycling, amalgamation, recuperation, synthesis, analogy: nothing more to it than that. Yesterday's news. Dreams will never give us one glimpse of the world without Nisard, quit your dreaming.

Threre's no hope of sanctuary, no refuge (I consider the dank crypt among cypress trees an uncompelling exception): Nisard is everywhere, omnipresent, if it's not him it's his spoor. One cannot exude boredom and mediocrity without soiling the floorboards a bit. His oozings form puddles that are not the sort that reflect the stars. This is how swamps are born. Pestilential, right from the start. Nisard is a very organized man, he never does things by half measures. The calamity is always total. Where to flee? Where to hide? A bear is already waiting in the nearest shelter.

I have hated others, I've hated Brossard, I've hated Distinguin, I've hated Chabrou, Zugari, Techer, I've hated Militrissa, they'd wronged me, they'd humiliated me (I've hated Opole), they'd deceived me (and I've hated Ania), I hated them to death, but

I would never have killed them, oh, I wouldn't have turned up my nose at some small act of vengeance, wouldn't have turned down the chance to slash their Achilles tendons, I wished them all manner of misfortunes and mishaps, Techer for instance, I would gladly have slipped an otitis germ under his pillow, or Zugari, fat Zugari, I would have laughed to see him with a broken nose, I would certainly have asked if he'd tripped and come down like a ton of bricks, and when I heard Chabrou's business was failing I wanted to sing, to dance, I who never sing or dance, and as soon as I was alone I gave myself over to that pleasure, and I also rejoiced in the thought of Militrissa's face savaged by the claws of time, the future seemed so full of promise back then, and there are others I've hated, and I hate them still, but those are only simmering little hatreds, resentful, inglorious, because I can't work up a proper disgust, impotent hatreds, spineless, shameful, no, this is the only hatred I'm proud of, my hatred for Nisard, something else altogether, the revolt of a gravely offended intelligence, a sudden shudder of vitality, an old instinct reawakening amid a new outlook on the world, a force growing inside me.

Librarians answer my pleas only to frustrate them. *A Milkmaid Succumbs* is not to be found in their holdings. They all mention the *History of French Literature*, which seems everywhere to have escaped the cleansing ravages of fire or water or indeed a deliberate mass pulping, a simple matter of maintenance, because life must go on and the corpses have to be hauled away now and then to free up some shelf space. You're a writer, you labor to rename the world, to untangle meanings; you're beaten down by ennui, despair, bitterness, but in your books you stand tall, your head high, transforming your allergies into allegories far lovelier than the usual eczematous inflammation, and then one fine day you find yourself more helpless than ever, deader than your dead ashes, in a tomb even colder than yours, a prisoner of Désiré Nisard's *History of French Literature*. Ambition punished: it's like something out of a fable by La Fontaine (a seventeenth-century writer).

But this morning the mailman, that messenger of the gods, that fleet-footed sprite, that bounding genie, in reality a tubby old gent—but I'm not lying: his very breath on the stairs is a zephyr— hands me a long envelope bearing the return address of the Library of Pales. The emotion of the moment is too great, I can't go on. Read it yourself, and I'll listen:

> *Dear Monsieur:*
> *In response to your letter, I am pleased to inform you that our library does indeed possess a collection of archives relating to the author in question. You may well find the book that you seek among them, though I make no promises on that score, as the archives have not yet been fully catalogued. If you would be so good as to schedule a visit, we will retrieve the files and boxes containing the relevant documents, currently in storage.*
> *Yours,* etc.,
> *G. Bordage, Head Librarian*

My giddiest joys, too, come to me courtesy of Nisard: one more cause for sorrow. I'm never so happy as when I glimpse a fresh opportunity to destroy him. Soon my very climaxes will be those of a hunter caressing his rifle. Open fire, boys! But no, there's a world of difference between Nisard and a freshly killed stag. He's not that little white rabbit now gone blood-red, nor that red fox bled white. All the same, the thought of owning a pack of fine hounds, which never much tempted me before, nor even crossed my mind, suddenly seems quite appealing. Tallyho and view halloo! With this I am made multiple, I follow all of Nisard's trails at once. No hope of escaping me now. I'll track him down, surround him, corner him, then I'll drop my horn and let my violin announce the kill, as it's so long been longing to do. My sense of smell has grown keener as well, though I take no pleasure in that, Nisard's scent has never been hard to detect, it was precisely to stop smelling him that I used to take long, barefoot walks in the snow, praying for a head cold: now that odor indisposes me all the more, it's overpowering, the nearer I come to him the greater my respiratory distress: one after another, I find my dogs asphyxiated along the path, most of them already dead, others convulsing in agony, desperately clawing at their own bloodied snouts. I was dreaming of a pack of hounds. And here it is decimated before my dream has even come to an end.

I'm used to painful awakenings. The first thought in the morning is always a chilling one. Whether the sky out the window be blue or gray, I know Nisard is beneath it, in the light. Today gray dominates. Nisard is at home in the clouds. My obnubilated eye soon spots his chubby-cheeked form among the cumulonimbus, the puffiest of them all, the darkest, the most bloated, the one the wind must struggle to push or drag through the skies, the one that slows, stops, settles in, its only movement henceforth an expansion: its own spew, plummeting earthward. Let it expand, I don't care. Today I'm going to Pales.

We're finally going to do battle, documentation in hand. I can well imagine some grumbling here and there (Nisard has so many allies who don't even know it!), I fully realize that certain of my attacks might be deemed excessive or ill-founded, I know there are those who consider me paranoid, or at the very least disturbed, witness this pathological fixation on an antediluvian literary critic, forever forgotten, his influence long since waned away. Well, now we're going to settle that question once and for all, on the basis of solid evidence. This time I have high hopes of getting my hands on *A Milkmaid Succumbs*, which will no doubt prove most instructive on the subject of that malign and underhanded gentleman, to whom, it's true, no one refers by name nowadays, but whose disseminated ideas mingle with the air around us just as the atoms of his decomposed corpse mingled with the earth—where did you think the bramble bush gets its vigor? If I so insistently cite his name, it's because there's nothing more noxious than smoke without fire, without origin or fixed abode. You imagine you're dispersing the fumes with a fan: they've simply clouded your mind. Nothing more pernicious than the unnamed virus. Once identified, it immediately becomes less fearsome, you can defend yourself, you can bombard it, we have toxins of our own to combat it, and potions of ground glass. Its name, let me remind you: Désiré Nisard.

Don't you see him at work all around you? On the side of crime, albeit with occasional backup from the police. Without descendants, and oddly eying your brood. Caned or velvet, the chair has thrown in its lot with him, bent to his rigid views, those are its knees you're sitting on. By what road will you flee him? He drove the paver (it's parked in front of his house). The odor of asphalt was simply the heady scent of his big hairy feet all along. Suddenly the allure of the desert becomes more understandable. But let us not forget: in the sand, every trail is a road. The horizon broadcasts the threat of his sudden appearance all around the world. Serenity shattered again! And so we flee into the mountains, only to find them ill-inclined to offer us refuge. The playing field is tilted in Nisard's favor: he might roll up at any moment. So what, then? Where? Not five minutes after you take up lodgings on the sea floor, the octopus already has you in its grasp, him again, Nisard, a ski-mask naïvely pulled over his face, his identity given away by those eight prehensile, constricting arms. You want to vanish into the forest? He grew up with the trees, he's fashioned a gibbet with your name on it among the birds' perches; and then, branching out, he encircles your neck with the very vines designed for simian gymnastics.

Unappetizing would be the black sausage prepared with Nisard's blood.

Unbecoming would be the shirt sewn from Nisard's skin.
Unwarming would be the sweater knitted of Nisard's whiskers.
Unsensible would be the shoes cut from Nisard's calluses.
Oh! That poor little girl born of his sperm!

PALES, MEDICINAL-PLANT CAPITAL OF FRANCE. A most
charming locale, as you can guess. Past the chamomile fields, the
town also has a painted cave, closed to the public, frequented only
by blind bats and cold worms; sometimes the odd prehistorian dis-
creetly slips through the entrance, as he might enter a brothel, and
indeed, not long after, his sharp little cries can be heard from outside. Forewarned of my arrival, Madame Bordage, the librarian—a
blonde brunette, thin, fat, cordial, gruff, young, old, check none
that apply—has laid out every Nisard-related document in her ar-
chives on a secluded little table. There's no lack of them. Nisard
left quite a paper trail on the cream-colored paper of his age. Will
I find *A Milkmaid Succumbs* among these volumes, bound in the
green leather of the calves of his age? Perhaps, in one of these large,
flat, black boxes held shut by straps, the manuscript of that work?
It'll take me hours to sort through all these papers, maybe days. So
much evidence, inevitably incriminating, to fill out the prosecuto-
rial brief I'm patiently compiling. I call my hotel before I sit down.
I tell them I'll be staying a week. Possibly longer, I add. Unhurried,
I return to the table laid for me. I stand motionless for a moment.
I don't touch a thing. This time I've got Nisard in my sights: let us
savor this moment. I can vividly picture the trembling buffoon,
back to the bullet-riddled library wall. I raise my rifle.

Finally I pick up the stack's topmost volume. A collection of critical writings by Barbey d'Aurevilly. Apathetic and assiduous, Madame Bordage has inserted a bookmark on the first page of a chapter devoted to Nisard. I take my time. Here and there my wandering eye lights on a mouthwatering snatch: . . . *there are certain hands that respect nothing . . . it was enough to raise shouts of "No more!" from anyone with the slightest reverence for beauty . . . was proclaimed "the poet of common sense" because he was the poet of vulgarity, two things all too often confused on our shores.* The grand style! Rare are the days that begin with such a welter of auspicious presages. There are some joys, then, that one would await in vain from chocolate, but which austere studies dispense in profusion. I go back to the beginning and settle in to read. Barbey's attacks are both lively and brilliant, I would find them infinitely delectable were they not in fact aimed, as I suddenly realize on seeing his name continually return as the subject of each sentence, at one François Ponsard, a dramatist of Nisard's time, who was unquestionably a great ass himself, but a perfectly inoffensive one, and who inspires in me an indifference scarcely troubled by the vague regret of not having had the opportunity to boo his plays, ineptly imitated from Corneille or Chénier, and rhythmically stamp the floorboards amid a band of cackling, jeering companions. But what matter! There are plenty of occasions for just such amusement today. More distressingly, Ponsard's name appears where I was expecting Nisard's, on each of the documents laid out for my perusal. Slapdash and fastidious, Madame Bordage must have inopportunely pulled out this box in lieu of the other, but, when I politely point out her error, she replies: Nisard, Ponsard, you're playing word games, dear

Monsieur, aren't they one and the same? I believe it was Ponsard you spoke of in your letter. I protest: Ponsard, no, certainly not, what's Ponsard to me, no, Nisard, Désiré Nisard! Now, now, she shoots back, let's not lose our temper, if Ponsard won't do I'll go see what we have on the other one, but really, she goes on mumbling as she walks away, Nisard or Ponsard, what's the difference, an ass and a hole in the ground . . . And then, after a brief absence, triumphant, all smiles, witless and witless, the librarian places the four volumes of the *History of French Literature* on the table before me. All you have to do is ask, she says.

CHARLOTTE, North Carolina (Reuters) – *Désiré Nisard offered another defense on Friday for his decision to go to war despite the UN inspectors' failure to find any trace of weapons of mass destruction.*

"We didn't find the weapons we were expecting to find, the weapons everyone thought would be there. But I know they had the capacity to produce such weapons. Knowing what I know today, I would have made the same decision," he stated.

The authors of a CIA report drafted for D. Nisard last July and made public this week predict that, in the best-case scenario, the instability will continue for some time to come; at worst, the country will slide into outright civil war.

Nisard trips on the top step of the massive staircase. He tumbles head over heels. His skull is split, his nose spurting blood. But his fall isn't over yet. Not so fast, still a long way to the bottom. A great many more steps to somersault over, and several tricky curves to negotiate. No doubt Nisard himself will be surprised to hear it, but the staircase's metal teeth crave his limp body—they sink into his flesh, they chew hungrily. And then crush his bones, to get at the marrow within. It's not hunger now: it's pure gluttony. Bouncing and sliding, the body pursues its descent, here comes the first turn, can he change course in time? It seems unlikely, it's not looking good, he'd have to brake somehow, slow himself down, no hope of that, a dark chasm lies open before him . . . then Métilde tugs at my sleeve: What, you've never seen the Eiffel Tower before?

I hate him, but I take care not to let my hatred blind me. I regularly return to the dictionary and its coolly objective definitions: *Narrow-minded, regressive, high-handedly pedantic, Nisard made an ideal candidate for the Académie Française; he was elected to that institution in 1850, defeating Alfred de Musset by a wide margin. The revolution of 1848 had put an end to his career as a Ministerial deputy and driven him from the sphere of public education, but after the coup d'état of December 1852 he regained all the lofty positions he had once held: he was named inspector general of higher education (March 1852), then secretary to the Council of Public Instruction; finally, he succeeded Villemain in the Chair of French Eloquence at the Faculté des Lettres. Little admired by his students, who rightly suspected him of servility to a deeply despised government and found his shifting political views repugnant, he first faced only muted hostility. It was in 1855 that the storm finally broke: in one of his lectures, he had the audacity to speak of two* separate moralities, one narrow and the other broad; the one, highly restrictive, governing the actions of simple private citizens, and the other, very lax, applying solely to princes who violate their oaths and extract millions from the Bank. No doubt he did not express himself quite so clearly as this, and the following day he protested that undue inferences had been drawn from his words; but such was indeed his opinion, visible behind his tortured circumlocutions, and indeed never once did he disavow the distinction between those two moralities. A torrent of hisses greeted this cynical assertion, and Monsieur Nisard soon found himself being escorted to his home amid a jeering throng not unreminiscent of a charivari, that display of popular merriment he had once found so good-hearted and so typically French. The magistrates' court brought charges against the uprising's ringleaders; after a trial that quickly revealed itself as the political event that it was, fifteen students were sentenced to several months' imprisonment. Monsieur Nisard was able to continue his classes only under the protection of numerous squads of city police; but soon, to reward him for braving a public outcry in his defense, Napoléon III named him Commander of the Legion of Honor (1856), then Director of the École Normale (1857). There, as at the Sorbonne, he aroused only antipathy among the student youth. In 1867, an admiring letter having been sent by a student to Sainte-Beuve, after the latter's spirited defense of freethinking before the Senate, Nisard succeeded in discovering the name of that noble act's initiator and had him expelled; a revolt ensued, and the École had to be temporarily shut down. Should we suspect Larousse himself of bias? Do we dare doubt the lexicographer's integrity? But we can easily test his reliability for ourselves. Let us for example turn to his definition of **CHAIR**: *seat fitted with a back, without arms*. Let us turn to his definition of **CEILING**: *flat, horizontal surface closing off the top of an enclosed space in a building*. I see nothing to add, and most importantly nothing to contest. The carpenter and the mason themselves could not be more objective in their concrete approach to these questions. Pierre Larousse's unbending impartiality was the sole guarantor of his undertaking's worth; if that virtue need be demonstrated yet again, then, I think, we may here rest our case.

My attacks are not always as devastating as I would like. Nisard holds his ground. My cudgel's cast-iron head cracks on encountering his unbreakable skull; I join my slender hands around his bull neck, praying in vain for a successful strangulation; my lightning bolts ricochet back and forth in his woodstove, warming his cadaverous flesh. So suppose I tried lulling him with love? Mollified by my caresses, he might prove more receptive to my lances and knives; if I could slip my hand beneath his leathery skin, full access would at long last be mine. I can see it now: I give his nerves a good pinch, with one fingernail I dig a canal to divert the flow of his blood and lymph. But first, shower him with affection, with loving attentions. Métilde, I'll be needing your beautiful eyes . . . this time I'm not the man for the job. Her answer is no. It's all up to me. Up to me to hold that hideous creature close, to spread my balm over his sensitive zones and gently massage, to finger his folds of fat. To sing his favorite songs into his ear. What a fine-looking young man you are, Désiré! You don't mind if I call you

Désiré? When I speak your name, Désiré, you must understand, that's my desire you're hearing.

A face of water trickling over my own, that's how I first learn to recognize you, Désiré, through my tears.

I can't look on you without weeping.

A purifying flood, a cleansing flood. My wolf mask has been washed away.

You never kept your beauty to yourself, as women do in mirrors, you wanted it to radiate, to spread far and wide. And in that enchantment grim winter turns to spring, and the bird that was only a hesitant lie of the dust is reborn.

No more friction. Copernicus was a prophet: now the globe that is our world does indeed turn. It needed your supple footstep to shift its load of stones.

So graceful, so lissome: you must have a cat concealed in every pocket, or if not, what hidden, well-oiled gears?

I want to know nothing more of this earth than the hazy landscapes that shimmer behind you.

I lose myself in the contemplation of your person.

I lose blood from my palms, pierced by my fingernails; I lose fingernails, gnawed by my teeth. How fragile I am, and how I fall apart in the contemplation of your person!

I can't go on. This is killing me.

I also love the lush curls of your muttonchop whiskers, thanks to which, one fine day, your quarter-profiles will inevitably meet nose to nose and devour each other.

I love your wide, hollow ears, else where would my garbage trucks dump their loads?

The olive's wizened wooden pit would be a brain too complex to sustain your rudimentary mechanism, so where did you get that olive complexion? Perhaps you've spent six months underwater?

This at least is true, Nisard: I can't look at you without weeping.

In 1878, the critic's astute pen expels the following funerary oration, worthy of his master Bossuet: "*This century has no need of poets. All the vitality of our age tends toward politics and industry, and it is to these that every worthy mind aspires. The time of poetry in France is past.*" While, oblivious to all this, Verlaine and Laforgue are naïvely inventing a new verse, while the invisible shock wave of the *Illuminations* and *Maldoror* is beginning to rattle the world, old Nisard, ten years from his death, proves, with the impeccable perspicacity I'm endeavoring to highlight in this book, that he has not lost his touch.

Bounding over the summits, the beautiful creature known as the izard or isard defies both gravity and vertigo—its delicate hoof strikes the rock, kindling a spark that ignites its rocket fuel, and so the sprite shoots skyward again, into thin air, its trajectory perfectly mirroring the moon's, or an arrow's. Its body is slender and muscular, its coat brown or rust depending on the season, its head proud, elegantly formed, topped with two short horns, slightly curved toward the rear. Adroit as any Italian paintbrush, its silken eyelash needs only one stroke to paint the round eye, dun and gold, beneath its bony brow. But no doubt this fearless, hardy creature would be happier in the rugged landscape that forms the painting's background. Its cloven hooves offer it a total of eight contact points with the ground, the sharp edges gripping firmly to both rock and ice, the elastic pads serving as springs, ever ready to release their tension. Prolonged, intensive exertion is mere child's play, thanks to its enormous heart. The isard can barrel down a steep hundred-yard slope in twenty seconds, then race up again just as fast. Its grace and agility, its prodigious leaps, its blazing sprints, its incessant acrobatics, its quicksilver antics and bounds make of the severe mountain an enchanting volcano, forever shooting out unpredictable projectiles. Nisard, as his name indicates: the negation of all that, with a capital *N*.

A milkmaid sucks cum, such is obviously the subliminal image hidden in the title of that ribald tale. I've absolutely got to get hold of it. I'm awakening my sleeper agents. Let the hunt begin! I've got all my men on the case. *A milkmaid sucks cum*. Pornography as wordplay. *Ma's milk sucked, I come*. So obviously Oedipus—him again!—has a hand in this thing. All his life, Désiré—born, need it be said, in a house on the Rue au Lait—must have sought to recapture the rapturous pleasures offered him by his mother Marie Scolastique Miel's breast. Poor man, pursuing that quest on literature's great flat body, and finding, by way of caresses and sweet nothings, of milk and honey, only rough paternal head-smacks and tongue-lashings: hence this attempt to script that fantasy of a lasting maternal love for himself. But soon, carried away by the intensity of his emotion, by the urges of his young body, he must have recognized the real desire behind that nostalgia, and abandoned himself to the incestuous longings thus revealed to his conscious mind, shamelessly unleashing the demons of his depravity, throwing himself ecstatically into the most lascivious descriptions, turning his poor mother over and over on the spring mattress of his sick imagination, I really would like to get my hands on that book, that book he would later disown, once his spunk pooled up in his slippers along with his blood, his middle-aged body now frigid as a ghost's. Doggedly I pursue my inquiries. I need that book, you understand, we need that book.

Nisard appeared at the apogee of western civilization, the child of its toils, the end result of every effort it expended since its first hesitant steps. Everything that was extracted, produced, and refined, century after century, on lathes or in alembics, by daring, single-minded, ingenious men, it all led to this, to that prototype, intended as the new norm. Painstakingly assembled, lovingly buffed, here is the finished object, the creation of man by man: Nisard! Was this the dream of the conquistadors, the pioneers, was it with one eye on that distant goal that the compass and sextant were devised? Were mathematics conceived solely to derive this formula for the ideal Earthling? Were French curves and rulers so tirelessly wielded, and so many candles burned in the cold night air, for the sole purpose of drawing up that sinister form? Did the Australopithecus defend its life against saber-toothed tigers and the rigors of the ice age to give birth, its labors finally at an end, to Désiré Nisard? Somewhere a miscalculation must have found its way into the plans. Where? When? What? Is it too late to make the necessary changes?

Is it too late to recalibrate, re-aim, hit Nisard in the heart? We'd be remiss if we didn't give it a shot. Here's my idea: wasting not a minute more, I'll make my way to Châtillon-sur-Seine, his birthplace, the very scene of the originary catastrophe—perhaps there's still time to nip that thug in the bud? No sooner do I speak the name of the relevant street than I am transported to the Rue Désiré Nisard, ex-Rue au Lait. The family home was destroyed along with the rest of the neighborhood during the bombardments of June 15, 1940. In its place, a row of sad, gray-doored garages: Man's adventure on earth ends here. But Nisard's ghost still wanders through the little town, which would nonetheless be only too happy to find him a successor in the role of local pride and joy—a role he performs less spellbindingly with each passing year—and finally offer the world, for example, a soccer player with a magical dribble. The *lycée* bears his name; in the entryway, the visitor is greeted by a drab portrait of the old man, no way to tell if it's the paint that's faded or if the thing's had that shabby look from the start, out of fidelity to its model. The attics of the municipal library exhibit the writing desk on which Nisard wasted so many reams of paper (note to self: come back with an axe). In the gardens of the town hall, finally, there still sits—atop a stone pedestal into which the two brothers, Charles and Auguste, are more modestly set, in the form of medallions—a tarnished bronze bust (tarnished from the start, out of fidelity to its model?) of Désiré, offered by the Nisard family and dedicated in 1895. On June 17, 1988, the centennial of his death, the town thought itself duty-bound to hold a "Désiré Nisard Day." A small handful of bystanders were thus able to hear a morning serenade performed before that monument by the Lyre Châtillonnaise, the town band, then an address delivered by Maurice Schumann himself, ex-Minister of Foreign Affairs, current member of the Académie Française: I would have given my eyeteeth to be there, to savor those wonderful moments. There are some regrets that nothing can assuage. Neither time nor amnesia will ever stanch the flow of my tears.

Nonetheless, my journey was not in vain. For, in addition to the magnificent Vix Krater, the jewel of its collections, the local museum is pleased to possess an assortment of documents and objects once owned by that child of the locality, now relegated to the cellars, it must be said, and rarely displayed. With unbounded good will and a touch of perplexity, the curator authorizes me to take stock of that treasure trove:

1) Carefully extracted from its sheath of wood and white leather, here is Désiré Nisard's senatorial saber, a beautiful parade weapon, hilt of gilded metal and mother-of-pearl, unsharpened acid-etched blade ornamented with an eagle, its wings outstretched.

2) Carefully extracted from its green leather case, here is Nisard's letter-opener, with a short, sharpened blade and a bone handle marked with the monogram D.N.

3) Carefully extracted from its black leather sleeve, here is Nisard's telescopic opera glass, which I clap to my eye, observing unsurprised that through it one sees neither very clearly nor very far.

4) In a cardboard box, on a plump little white satin cushion, here are Nisard's two medals: the gilt cross of the Legion of Honor, struck in the center with the effigy of Napoleon I, and the violet moiré ribbon of the Commander of the Order of Leopold of Belgium, from which hangs a white enamel cross bearing in its center the figure of a standing lion and the device *In Unity, Strength*. Alas, missing from this collection is Désiré's first decoration, perhaps the only one he legitimately earned, his celebrated necklace of apples.

5) Another box contains Nisard's tarnished bronze senatorial medallion, also stamped with an emblem—is it the lion? Oh no! it's the eagle, flattened like a fly.

6) I also don the pair of spectacles, with tinted lenses and a delicate frame, that the curator has taken from a pine box, observing unsurprised that through them one sees neither very clearly nor very far.

7) The museum further houses a white handkerchief embroidered with an *N*, a gray silk scarf checked with thin black lines (three feet by three)—rather elegant, I must admit, if somewhat carelessly crumpled—and a pair of beige fingerless gloves of ribbed wool in a highly dilapidated state: what's next, the unveiling of Nisard's underclothes?

8) No: apart from a clutch of illegible handwritten letters— the tangled thread of Nisard's thought—and a few newspaper

clippings of no interest, only one last item remains (but what an item!): the highlight of that extraordinary collection.

9) Nisard's Académie Française habit, more black than green, laden with braid, cords, and gilded stripes: only the aged majorette who insists on leading a parade of nubile young girls, or the sad circus barker dubbed, in French, "Monsieur Loyal," could don that costume without compounding the already consummate preposterousness of their attire, adding only the weight—assuredly burdensome—of those embroideries, those buttons, those plaited cords, those epaulets: and now the galumphing majorette can no longer hurl her baton, and now Monsieur Loyal is no longer quick enough on his feet to leave the ring before the tigers come on. And will Nisard himself someday lose his gift for doing harm? It was nonetheless to him that the Académie Française awarded, in 1881, its Grand Biennial Prize, in recognition of "the body of work best suited to honor our country"! While the fat majorette weeps amid laughter and jeers! While the rubicund joviality of Monsieur Loyal fades between the tiger's jaws! *The body of work best suited to honor our country*!

I'll find lots of elbow room in the book without Nisard, I'll have free run of the place. I settle in with an African elephant, that one at least will be spared. No quarters could be so uncramped. My arms can grow. My legs, especially, lengthen. I never knew so much space could exist. That will be my bedroom over there, and here the kitchen, and there the living room. Would you excuse me for a moment, I'm just going for a little sprint, be right back. A little sprint, why a little sprint? I've got a saddled horse right here, puffing and stamping and ready to take off at full gallop. In a trice, I can be a mere dot on the horizon—the horizon, disencumbered at last!—in the book without Nisard. There's room for snow, too, all the snow (and we all know how much room snow takes up). Why not come with me? There's so much to discover, so much Nisard was concealing from view, so much to do that Nisard's baleful presence forbade. Now he's gone, and all of a sudden our bodies are lighter—so it wasn't our bones that were weighing us down, and not the heavens either.

Among Nisard's possessions preserved in the museum of Châtillon, my curiosity was also piqued by

10) A wax-paper envelope containing some twenty large peppercorns.

Found in the Academician's pocket, the curator confided. A mystery. We swapped a few quips on pepper's supposed aphrodisiac properties. A stimulant for a flagging old man? A little something to spice up his love life? In hopes of reviving his ardor, a grimacing Nisard crunches the black grains while Élisabeth fingers the limp violet ribbon of the Commander, smiling wistfully at the lion in the cross, upright on its rear legs, haloed with its flamboyant mane. A domestic scene sadly absent from the slender catalogue of engravings and portraits of Nisard, depicted at all ages and in all the most becoming poses of the orator or man of letters, which I brought home from my pilgrimage to Châtillon and now sullenly leaf through: that severe mouth's grim rictus is contagious. Reaching the last pages, I glance idly over the bibliography—and suddenly, blinding joy. *In July 1834,* it informs me, casual as can be, *Désiré Nisard publishes a brief romance entitled* A Milkmaid Succumbs *in the* Revue de Paris. A revelation! So it never appeared as a separate volume at all! Those attempts to expunge it were thus doomed from the start. If Nisard was hoping to inflame my bloodhounds' sinuses with that pepper stuffed into his pockets, he's out of luck: the complete leather-bound collection of the *Revue de Paris* can be found in any library worth its salt. I now hold in my hands volume seven, from the year 1834. The table of contents lists Chapter 4 of Balzac's *Séraphîta, Claude Gueux* by Victor Hugo, *Le Château de Vaux* by Léon Golzan, a review by Victor Schoelcher of Jules Ziegler's *Eloa, la soeur des anges,* miscellaneous works by a few others, now forgotten—Auguste Pichard, the Marquis de Salvo, Fresnel, Antoni Deschamps, Louis de Maynard, Jules Vernière, M. L. Aymar—and, on page 213, my friends, *A Milkmaid Succumbs,* by Désiré Nisard.

"*In the first days of May, while visiting the countryside a few leagues from Paris, I heard the village church bell vigorously pealing early one morning.*" Thus opens Désiré Nisard's lascivious tale. From the start, the most vile pornography. The bells are announcing the burial of the little milkmaid who passed by the vacationing narrator's door every morning. "*To think of a young girl dying on such a beautiful sunny day, the first fine day of the year! Dying when everything is being born, when everything lives anew, when everything is singing! Dying when all the leaves are once again fluttering on the trees, when not a single flower has yet withered, and when the first flowers to wither will be those placed on her grave!—And I found myself weeping, as if this girl were my sister."* I will forgive any delicate reader who prefers to skip over these lines: one has the right to protect one's private domain from external pollutions, to refuse to allow an erotomaniac's sordid fantasies to infect the healthy caprices of a free and inventive personal sexuality. I myself must persist, for such is my mission, and the study of Nisard's dirty laundry will have much to tell us of his true nature, at bottom. *"The birds were singing in the trees; the air was gently stirred by that morning breeze which blows from one never quite knows where, and which seems the breath of an awakening earth; hidden behind the chestnut trees, the sun pierced their leaves, still small and sparse, with a thousand beams, dappling me with light and shadow."* That tiger in a frock coat thus attends the funeral of said milkmaid, *"a rosebud never given the chance to bloom."* Droolingly, he describes the virginal cortege of young girls escorting the casket: *"their dewy cheeks, their sweet, impassive faces, displaying more pleasure in being dressed up for a special occasion than sorrow at accompanying their older friend to her last resting place—in my emotion, I found myself dreaming of them as angels, come down from on high to rescue another of their number from her earthly exile . . . Only at intervals, when their unequal paces divided the white crowd of young girls, could the head of the coffin be seen moving forward in its stiff and angular way, or, at the other end, its foot emerging from the crowd; I say 'head' and 'foot,' for which is the more dead and inert, the coffin or the body? But save those rare moments when death showed its face beneath these disguises, it was only a white mass of living beings and flowers, like young girls in festival dress bearing as their angel some child crowned with immortelles and clad in roses.*" As this carnival parade creeps toward the cemetery, we are given an exhaustive account of the dead girl's sorrowful story. Smitten with a young man whom her father found too impecunious to make a suitable husband, the little milkmaid succumbed to her grief. Our narrator—"voyeur" would be the more accurate term—then preens himself on having not long before witnessed a silent rendezvous of the two lovers, sitting side by side in a forest glade, transfixed with passion, exchanging long, languorous gazes but never once touching. Here I refuse to explicitly cite the words Nisard so carefully chose to depict that sordid encounter: they'll turn your stomach. This covert tryst became known to the milkmaid's father, a hateful, grasping brute, who reprimanded her severely. She would not survive that confrontation. "*Stricken, she took to her bed . . . Two days later, the illness had progressed with great swiftness, and the fever was so high that a doctor was summoned . . . But so rapidly was her ailment advancing that after the doctor they were forced to call for the priest.*" There follow a few scabrous scenes at the young girl's deathbed. " *'Too late!' she sighed . . . She was sinking faster and faster; her agitations had ceased, the tranquility of death was beginning.*" Nisard prolongs the death-throes well beyond the endurance of the poor milkmaid—now a buttermaid, what with all these churning emotions. A certain cheesiness creeps into the scene, and Nisard licks his chops, like a hyena scenting a fine feast in the offing. The despairing swain is allowed to pay one last call on his beloved. "*She saw him not; her eyes had already closed, never to open again.*" At long last, the Camembert's in the can! "*Her soul was adrift in that night which, for the Christian, precedes the eternal day . . . Kneeling at the foot of the bed, the young man's wrenching sobs drowned out the holy prayers. He kept her hand pressed to his cheek, and at length he felt it going cool, that hand that not long before was still warm"*— even today we still laugh at old Jacques de la Palice thanks to just such an idiotic remark: "fifteen minutes before he died he was still alive." *"He raised his eyes and saw that the end had come. He fled the room, wailing in despair."* All too clearly can we picture the panting writer scrawling out these lines, sweating and flushed, his clothing scandalously undone. The cortege finally reaches its destination, an opportunity for Nisard to offer up some somber ruminations on the brevity of our earthly lives, and to boldly affirm that a cemetery is a gloomy place. *"The diurnal birds, the singing birds, the birds that make love in broad daylight, such birds flee cemeteries. In order to attract them, a true city of the dead must be built, with broad promenades for the survivors, and tall leafy trees to whose shadows fine young ladies and their lovers will retire, reawakening their jaded souls and rousing themselves to earthly pleasure with the spice of a few brief thoughts of death."* As Nisard shamelessly abandons himself to these necrophilic musings, the young virgin's body is lowered into the grave. One last painfully theatrical scene pits the unworthy father against the disconsolate lover, then Nisard brings his tale briskly to a close: *"This was less than three months ago. The father died of an apoplectic fit on learning of the loss of a certain sum of money. The young man went off to live in Paris, where he has now married. The only flowers on the young girl's grave are the few wilted cornflowers I placed there."*

So it was this wilted cornflower, these fifteen mawkish pages, that Nisard strove so mightily to expunge—for the purpose, let there be no doubt, of fostering scandalous rumors, of concocting a mystery that would soon grow to a legend, hoping to palm off that anodyne twaddle as something twisted and foul, the howl of a damned soul; while the Marquis de Sade and the Comtesse de Ségur innocuously swat each other's behinds, one noble to another, this genuinely ignoble beast is lashing a naked child with a cobra, or sucking the soul from a freshly confessed dying man by means of a straw thrust into his eye. Even more calculating than I imagined, Nisard was counting on absence and invisibility to make a name for himself, fully aware that his many published works would never earn him glory, nor any other acclaim than the stifled yawns of a handful of students engaged in a titanic struggle to keep one eye open. But there at last is the truth about *A Milkmaid Succumbs*, a sentimental tale knitted with the crudest stuff of the Romanticism so in vogue at the time, using up the whole ball of yarn, such that Nisard's kitten has nothing left to play with but the little cardboard spool (another life made the poorer at his hands).

The more entire our knowledge of Nisard, the deeper our revulsion. If my contempt was a mill, Nisard would be all the wheat in France. There is no corner of that face on which we might pin our gaze without disgust. If he had just once in his life put a little overturned ladybug back on its feet, I would unhesitatingly sing his fingertip's praises. I would have devoted the bulk of these pages to his fingertip, so naturally inclined am I to celebration and tenderness. This book would have been a reliquary for Nisard's fingertip, all gold and sparkling gems. It would have been nothing but that. If he had once in his life put an overturned ladybug back on its feet, I would have made myself the herald of that noble act. The grateful ladybug would have sung through my voice:

Supine, afeard,
Beneath a tree—
Nisard appeared
And righted me

Or

I fear the grave
Cannot be far
But wait! I'm saved!
Thanks to Nisard

Or

The howling blizzard
Knocked me over
Then came Nisard
Now I'm in clover

Clearly I had a fine collection of heartfelt little verses in me, and that one single gesture on Nisard's part would have sufficed to make of this book something very different from what it is. But how can we think him even capable of such concern for the suffering world around him? He'd rather be interring milkmaids, that at least brings some comfort! That at least distracts Nisard from his own morose company. He won't put the little dead girl back on her feet either: we're all just insects to him. He faithfully accompanies us to our final abode. He assures himself that the stone slab has been well sealed over our grave, lovingly dug just for us. He cements the joints with his own hands. He waits for the flowers to wilt on the tomb before heading off, just to be sure we don't find a way out. That's what Nisard calls compassion. It wasn't enough for him to dig literature's grave with his great shovel-like paws. Is that a pretty milkmaid passing by his window, humming a merry air? He won't give up until he's stuffed her into a filthy hole where she's clearly not going to get over her heartache, where her dewy complexion will soon lose its bloom, so irrefutably true is it that to die is simply to age all the more. You give him a cup of fresh, foamy milk, and what does Nisard do? Puts a fly in it.

He's a fly himself, endlessly buzzing, endlessly laying eggs! Oh, I know how he dotted his *i*s all right! Perhaps you remember that Grimm's fairy tale, "The Brave Little Tailor"? I'd like to be that sure-handed, sharp-eyed hero. I don't have a rag close at hand. No matter, my belt will do. It has a steel buckle. It whistles through the air overhead like a whirling flock of birds. Then suddenly swoops down onto the tiny, black-haired monster . . . Nizzzzzard crackles on my desk for a few moments longer. With the tip of my pencil (when may I expect a reliquary, all gold and sparkling gems, for the tip of my pencil?), I very kindly attempt to put him back on his feet. "Too late!" sighed the maiden. My bitter laughter drowns out the holy prayers. Right, chuck him out!

As an Academician, Larousse bravely continues, a crumpled handkerchief pressed to his nostrils, *Monsieur Nisard was chosen to respond to the inaugural addresses of several new inductees (Ponsard, the Duc de Broglie, Monsieur Saint-René de Taillandier), and never did any eloquence so gray and so drab envelop an audience, never did a more stifling blanket of tedium ever descend from the cupola of the Institut de France. Welcoming a man of letters into the Académie, Monsieur Nisard always seems to be handing out some school prize, or rebuking a refractory pupil: he gravely advised Ponsard to reread Boileau. Responding to the Duc de Broglie, who had emphatically praised Louis-Philippe: "I would be a most pitiable soul," cried Monsieur Nisard, "if I were discomfited by that praise. I loved, I served the Monarchy of 1830." His colleagues' glacial silence before this monotonous orator's clumsy reminder that he had thrived equally under every successive French government, and had been granted honors by all manner of different régimes, was for Monsieur Nisard a harsh lesson, and one he learned well. His speech on the inauguration of Monsieur Saint-René de Taillandier was of a purely literary bent; there he returned, pompous as ever, to his overblown theories on the seventeenth century, declaring that "the most beautiful period of French literature is the age when France imitated no one." A very curious assertion to make about the age that in fact most imitated the Greeks, the Romans, and even the Spanish. But Monsieur Nisard would never give up on that notion.* Published in 1879, Pierre Larousse's *Great Universal Dictionary* is naturally silent on the last nine years of Nisard's life, but those latter words nevertheless summarize them perfectly: he wouldn't give up. His final work, *Considerations on the French Revolution and Napoleon*

I (1887), makes a depressing epilogue for an existence vainly devoted to shadows and regrets. He died in 1888 at San Remo, Italy, where his octogenarian carcass was warming itself: on the morning of March 25, the sun forgot about him, its services required by the burgeoning spring, and the cold confiscated that bag of old bones.

Extracts from a posthumous homage to Désiré Nisard by Charles Bigot, published April 7, 1888, in the Revue Bleue:

Monsieur Désiré Nisard died last week. Born in 1806, he was the eldest member of the Académie Française. He was still full of life when he died. I do not come to judge the writer that he was, nor the critic and historian of French literature: I wish to speak of the man. I lived for three years in the company of Monsieur Nisard, and will endeavor to paint him as he appears in my memories, retaining all my independence of spirit, but never forgetting the respect that I owe him.

It was in 1860, upon my arrival at the École Normale Supérieure, that I met Monsieur Nisard, then head of that school. A most severe discipline reigned within those walls. The monitors—the "caimans," as we called them—never took their eyes off us. Detention on Thursdays and Sundays, our two free days, was a common occurrence. Woe unto him who lingered in bed one minute too many, to him who chatted with a neighbor in study hall; woe especially unto him who allowed himself to be caught secretly smoking a pipe or cigarette! And yet Monsieur Nisard had greatly relaxed the disciplinary code of the establishment. It was permitted to talk in the refectory;

curfew on our days off was set back by an hour. Monsieur Nisard desired nothing so much, I believe, as to be a popular headmaster. Did he succeed? Was he the beloved figure he so longed to be? It must be said: he was not. Monsieur Nisard spared no effort in his eagerness to charm us and win us over. When we knocked at his door to request some small favor, he did not often grant the favor requested, but he had exquisite ways of refusing. He liked to familiarly take a pupil's arm, as if it were that of a close friend. Alas! Nothing came of these gestures; all Monsieur Nisard's amiability and graciousness was in vain. Every one of us, or nearly, looked on him only with quiet hostility and an insurmountable ill will. This had two causes.

First, there were Monsieur Nisard's literary doctrines. We who read Victor Hugo in private, we who spent our vacations devouring the novels of George Sand and all manner of modern writing, we knew full well that our teachers' lofty disdain for the literature of our century was unfounded. It was to such writers that we owed our profoundest emotions, our most soaring ardors, our keenest intellectual pleasures; we simply let our teachers say what they like, quietly dismissing them as "relics." And as it happened Monsieur Nisard was not only a fervent devotee of the classics, but the most rigid and single-minded of all such devotees. We students rarely read his History of French Literature; if we did, it was more to find arguments against its author than in his favor. We were fond of citing two or three historical slips he made in those pages, errors we found perfectly hilarious. No one created fewer lovers of the classics than the lover of the classics that was Monsieur Nisard, the head of the École Normale. Two simple details will tell us more than the most exhaustive analysis: for one, Michelet's History of France was removed from the library on the grounds that it made dangerous reading; for another, one of my fellow students was punished for bringing an issue of the Revue des Deux Mondes into school.

But to our minds this was not Monsieur Nisard's gravest misdeed; politics alienated us from him still more than literature. We were nearly all Republicans. Monsieur Nisard was a Bonapartist: that was his unforgivable crime, that was what stripped him of all authority in our eyes. After the coup d'état, the Empire had named him Monsieur Villemain's successor at the Sorbonne. There an unfortunate blunder had earned him the nickname "Nisard of the two moralities" among the students. Monsieur Nisard had offered certain somewhat overindulgent reflections on the authority of the State. The Dean, Victor Leclerc, who was not fond of him, and whose tongue was notoriously sharp, curtly interrupted: "Enough, Monsieur Nisard; I will not have it said that two separate moralities may be affirmed here in the heart of the Sorbonne." Whence the nickname, which he was never able to shake off.

One fine day, the Sorbonne's great hall, where to his sorrow Monsieur Nisard had chosen to lecture, was, most unusually, packed to the rafters; all the student youth had come out to protest. Forewarned, the police had come along to maintain order. Informers made chalk marks on the backs of the loudest protestors; at the end of the class, the gendarmes arrested them in the street. They were jailed. Monsieur Nisard willingly left the Sorbonne for the position of director of the École Normale, less prone to such tumult. The École Normale was not allowed to display its political opinions; it had nonetheless consented to do just that. We forgave Monsieur Nisard neither his past volte-faces nor his present zeal. He kept a marble *bust of Napoleon I on his office mantelpiece. He published miscellanies in the* Journal Officiel. *Morality was for him above all a matter of propriety, of good breeding. An insufficient morality, I admit; an unstable morality, accepting of many grave faults, and allowing a great many compromises. Rather than any nobler cause, we preferred to attribute his Caesarism to sheer self-interest. We knew he was a candidate for the Senate. With every new list of senate appointments published in the* Journal Officiel, *we noted with spiteful glee that Monsieur Nisard had been passed over yet again.*

As for his History of French Literature, *it is a narrow-minded and incomplete book to be sure, but it is a book all the same. Its greatest failing is its systematic turn of mind, its insistence on reducing all things to one single notion, one single theory. But not everyone is capable of such a failing.*

This, then, was Monsieur Nisard, the head of the École Normale; these are the reasons—to say nothing of his elegant mind—for which he has remained a beloved and respected figure in my eyes. What profit I could have drawn from his sage teachings, if only man were able to profit from an experience other than his own!

Here, it would seem, lies ample delight for that lover of funeral orations, himself a highly gifted deplorer. Listen to his heart-rending wail: "*I know that it is no longer the custom to travel down the Rhône to Arles, since that noble city does not lie on the road to Marseille.*" How not to be moved to tears by this lament? Not even the irreparable decline of French literature tormented Nisard like this landlubberly nostalgia. Rather than bury him in the family crypt like a common milkmaid, it would have been an inspired idea to send his corpse floating down the river in a wicker cradle. Imagine the frail barque waiting patiently at the locks, speeding along when the current picks up, now running into the bank, re-launched by a tow-horse with a compassionate kick of its hind legs, navigating among the barges with their more precious cargo of coal or hay, sometimes capsizing, of course, then drifting into stagnant backwaters with the bloated corpses of drowned dogs and muskrats, drydocked for long stretches on a sandbar, pulled back into the current by a rise in the water level, a lightweight recumbent sculpture tanned by the sun and the rain, green as a water lily and indeed considered as such by the frogs, who know a thing or two about water lilies, now pulling alongside the skiff of a fisherman coincidentally just out of worms for his hooks, who thanks this Samaritan with a caress of his oar, floating on day and night, grimacing in the reflected moonlight, and finally reaching the home port of Arles, where the sawmill's young apprentices deploy their boathooks to guide him and the other tree trunks toward the whirling blades, where our imagination prefers to lose sight of him.

Whether ash or radioactive sawdust, while oblivion submerged Nisard's memory as peaceful night quells the last gleams of the day, his powdery residue, borne on the wind, insinuated itself into even the most solid objects, jammed up the joints that link man to his world, gangrened the living tissue that is rubber, finally settled over all things and corroded all things, invaded the vital principle of all

things, the disrupted logic of all things, and the disturbed consciousness of men, inducing the spasms and sneezing fits they so unjustly
attribute to pollen or a cat's batting eyelashes or the changing phases
of the moon. But this is in fact how Nisard outlasted himself, how
his influence lived on, unstoppable because unidentified, undefined:
and while it was child's play to bash that puppet Nisard on the head
with a stick, his ghost is not so easily grasped, much less pummeled,
and it's his ghost who sometimes passes a mocking hand through
your hair, mussing it, and who's laughing then?

I've often spotted Nisard, shaped out of snow or clay, sculpted in
marble or wood, cast in bronze, better put together than he ever
was in his lifetime, or vociferating at lecterns and pulpits with the
eloquence he so sorely lacked back when he himself struggled to
find his words. What aplomb he now has, and what vigor! His
scowl drifts from one face to the next. He is the sting of the nettle
and the asp at our feet. Often he possesses a youthful body, and
charms you with his wiles. For three weeks I thought of nothing
but his thighs, my hand under the sheet dreamed it was under his
skirt. Whence my wariness, expanding without end, sparing no
one. But in fact I truly believe everyone is infected. That ferment
is in our very cellars. The wine that intoxicates us also delivers our
nodding heads into the waiting hands of Nisard.

UGANDA (AFP) – *The Uganda Wildlife Authority has announced
the death of seven elephants, slaughtered by an ivory trafficker in*

Murchison Falls National Park. This brutal massacre of ten adults and one calf is the worst case of poaching in Uganda for more than twenty years.

The investigation is focused on a French national, Désiré Nisard, who was recently apprehended peddling what appeared to be freshly harvested tusks in the area of Kampala airport. Ugandan police are currently questioning the suspect.

Métilde is finding me increasingly irritable, foul-tempered, brusque. This very morning, I lashed out at an adolescent who was bellowing into his telephone at the next table in a café. "Suppose you emerged from adolescence right this instant?" I said. "Come on, give it a shot! Right now! Chop-chop! Let's go! Emerge! Leave your adolescence behind! Stick your head out, that's the first step. You're not planning to spend your whole life as this idiotic, noisy adolescent, are you, with your pants down around your knees and a language of twelve words to say everything there is to be said, that's not really your plan, is it? Suppose you decided right now to be done with adolescence? That's my suggestion: what do you say? This seems to me the ideal moment. I must admit, it would suit my companion and me very nicely, we'd like a little peace and quiet, we'd be most grateful if you'd take that leap without further ado, come on, shut off that phone, pull up your pants, and go buy a French language manual . . ." The adolescent understood not a word of all this, of course, he stayed right where he was, an incurable case of adolescence, though he did lower his voice a hair. It was Métilde who seemed angry. "Watch out," she told me, "you're getting to be every bit as odious as Nisard. You've been after him for so long, you're becoming just like him."

Becoming Nisard! Is it a curse? Is it fate? Is this Nisardification inscribed in the arc of every human existence? Is it an irresistible metamorphosis? Just another phase in the cycle? Its endpoint, perhaps? Or is it merely a sort of measles that begins by attacking the ears? An acute form of depression, of neurasthenia, of paranoia? An incurable neurosis? Is it simply the first sign of aging, when our era suddenly seems foreign to us, intolerable, and our body recoils like a leaf in the fire, shrinking and twisting, and as it recoils is hideously deformed, disfigured, becoming Nisard? Must we grant that Désiré Nisard merely incarnated that sad decline, shamelessly, even proudly, that abdication to which we must all eventually resign ourselves? Did he bravely shoulder his hideous destiny from the start? Is Nisard, in short, Christ, the true Christ, abjuring the heroic poses of the way of the cross, definitively mediocre, delighting in his limitations, secreting his own shell, and, coiled within it, still salivating over himself?

No, Métilde tells me, that's the Christ of the snails you're talking about. Nevertheless, the question remains: are we all doomed to become Nisard? Or is it simply because I've evoked this hypothesis that I feel my marrow slowly petrifying? My eyesight dims, I can scarcely see beyond the circle circumscribed by my arm. Only once every two or three days now do I lay a tiny egg that contains me, and my milk's going dry as well. My teeth are sharp but my gums are flabby, and when I chew, I chew myself. And very bitter to the taste I am. Becoming Nisard . . . The wheels begin to turn. Becoming Nisard. Yes, that just might be the answer.

I'm back in Châtillon-sur-Seine, but this time under cover of darkness. The night is fair and pitch-black, just the thing. Still, I'm sure the moon would have liked to see all this. The shutter gives way, then the window, here I am on the premises. I turn on my flashlight. I get my bearings. I orient myself. I know this place well. A narrow spiral staircase corkscrews unimpeded through the strata of times gone by, swift as a playground slide, and deposits me in the basement storeroom. In no time I locate the cabinet where Nisard's effects are stored. Less than three minutes later, I've draped myself in his costume, his Académie Française habit. It fits me—sad to say, but it fits me. You might think it was custom-tailored. I pull on the ugly fingerless gloves. I knot the gray scarf around my neck. I put on the tinted glasses. Then I stuff the opera glass, the letter-opener, the medallion, the handkerchief into my pockets. I pin the cross of the Legion of Honor to my chest, alongside the ribbon of the Commander of the Order of Leopold. To one side of my belt I attach the sheathed senatorial sword. Finally, I empty the envelope of peppercorns into my cupped hand, hesitate for a moment, and shove them into my mouth.

I slip out as I slipped in. How simple everything is from here on! My steps make scarcely a sound in the empty streets. Such tranquility! My shadow glides over the walls; sometimes a shop window fleetingly gives me a clearer view of the sour old man. I walk on the banks of the murmuring Douix, whose source lies just outside town. There a little natural pool has formed, and around it the village has installed a few benches. I sit down under a willow. The darkness is already less inky. I've pulled the ceremonial sword from its sheath and laid it on my knees. Just to see, I press the point to my breast and give a little push. But I'm not going to offer the senator a samurai's death. The first birdsong makes itself heard, then a very slight splash. A radiant dawn is rising over the world. Désiré Nisard sinks into the green waters.

ERIC CHEVILLARD was born in 1964 in La Roche-sur-Yon in the west of France. He published his first novel, *Mourir m'enrhume* (Dying Gives Me a Cold), at the age of twenty-three, and has since gone on to publish more than twenty other works of fiction, including *The Crab Nebula*, *On the Ceiling*, and *Palafox*.

JORDAN STUMP is the noted translator of numerous modern French novelists, including Nobel Prize winner Claude Simon. His translation of Simon's *Le Jardin des Plantes* won the French-American Foundation's Translation Prize.

SELECTED DALKEY ARCHIVE PAPERBACKS

SELECTED DALKEY ARCHIVE PAPERBACKS

CARLOS FUENTES, *Christopher Unborn.*
   Distant Relations.
   Terra Nostra.
   Where the Air Is Clear.
JANICE GALLOWAY, *Foreign Parts.*
   The Trick Is to Keep Breathing.
WILLIAM H. GASS, *Cartesian Sonata*
   and Other Novellas.
   Finding a Form.
   A Temple of Texts.
   The Tunnel.
   Willie Masters' Lonesome Wife.
GÉRARD GAVARRY, *Hoppla! 1 2 3.*
   Making a Novel.
ETIENNE GILSON,
   The Arts of the Beautiful.
   Forms and Substances in the Arts.
C. S. GISCOMBE, *Giscome Road.*
   Here.
   Prairie Style.
DOUGLAS GLOVER, *Bad News of the Heart.*
   The Enamoured Knight.
WITOLD GOMBROWICZ,
   A Kind of Testament.
KAREN ELIZABETH GORDON,
   The Red Shoes.
GEORGI GOSPODINOV, *Natural Novel.*
JUAN GOYTISOLO, *Count Julian.*
   Exiled from Almost Everywhere.
   Juan the Landless.
   Makbara.
   Marks of Identity.
PATRICK GRAINVILLE, *The Cave of Heaven.*
HENRY GREEN, *Back.*
   Blindness.
   Concluding.
   Doting.
   Nothing.
JIŘÍ GRUŠA, *The Questionnaire.*
GABRIEL GUDDING,
   Rhode Island Notebook.
MELA HARTWIG, *Am I a Redundant*
   Human Being?
JOHN HAWKES, *The Passion Artist.*
   Whistlejacket.
ALEKSANDAR HEMON, ED.,
   Best European Fiction.
AIDAN HIGGINS, *A Bestiary.*
   Balcony of Europe.
   Bornholm Night-Ferry.
   Darkling Plain: Texts for the Air.
   Flotsam and Jetsam.
   Langrishe, Go Down.
   Scenes from a Receding Past.
   Windy Arbours.
KEIZO HINO, *Isle of Dreams.*
KAZUSHI HOSAKA, *Plainsong.*
ALDOUS HUXLEY, *Antic Hay.*
   Crome Yellow.
   Point Counter Point.
   Those Barren Leaves.
   Time Must Have a Stop.
NAOYUKI II, *The Shadow of a Blue Cat.*
MIKHAIL IOSSEL AND JEFF PARKER, EDS.,
   Amerika: Russian Writers View the
   United States.
GERT JONKE, *The Distant Sound.*
   Geometric Regional Novel.
   Homage to Czerny.
   The System of Vienna.

JACQUES JOUET, *Mountain R.*
   Savage.
   Upstaged.
CHARLES JULIET, *Conversations with*
   Samuel Beckett and Bram van
   Velde.
MIEKO KANAI, *The Word Book.*
YORAM KANIUK, *Life on Sandpaper.*
HUGH KENNER, *The Counterfeiters.*
   Flaubert, Joyce and Beckett:
   The Stoic Comedians.
   Joyce's Voices.
DANILO KIŠ, *Garden, Ashes.*
   A Tomb for Boris Davidovich.
ANITA KONKKA, *A Fool's Paradise.*
GEORGE KONRÁD, *The City Builder.*
TADEUSZ KONWICKI, *A Minor Apocalypse.*
   The Polish Complex.
MENIS KOUMANDAREAS, *Koula.*
ELAINE KRAF, *The Princess of 72nd Street.*
JIM KRUSOE, *Iceland.*
EWA KURYLUK, *Century 21.*
EMILIO LASCANO TEGUI, *On Elegance*
   While Sleeping.
ERIC LAURRENT, *Do Not Touch.*
HERVÉ LE TELLIER, *The Sextine Chapel.*
   A Thousand Pearls (for a Thousand
   Pennies)
VIOLETTE LEDUC, *La Bâtarde.*
EDOUARD LEVÉ, *Suicide.*
SUZANNE JILL LEVINE, *The Subversive*
   Scribe: Translating Latin
   American Fiction.
DEBORAH LEVY, *Billy and Girl.*
   Pillow Talk in Europe and Other
   Places.
JOSÉ LEZAMA LIMA, *Paradiso.*
ROSA LIKSOM, *Dark Paradise.*
OSMAN LINS, *Avalovara.*
   The Queen of the Prisons of Greece.
ALF MAC LOCHLAINN,
   The Corpus in the Library.
   Out of Focus.
RON LOEWINSOHN, *Magnetic Field(s).*
MINA LOY, *Stories and Essays of Mina Loy.*
BRIAN LYNCH, *The Winner of Sorrow.*
D. KEITH MANO, *Take Five.*
MICHELINE AHARONIAN MARCOM,
   The Mirror in the Well.
BEN MARCUS,
   The Age of Wire and String.
WALLACE MARKFIELD,
   Teitlebaum's Window.
   To an Early Grave.
DAVID MARKSON, *Reader's Block.*
   Springer's Progress.
   Wittgenstein's Mistress.
CAROLE MASO, *AVA.*
LADISLAV MATEJKA AND KRYSTYNA
   POMORSKA, EDS.,
   Readings in Russian Poetics:
   Formalist and Structuralist Views.
HARRY MATHEWS,
   The Case of the Persevering Maltese:
   Collected Essays.
   Cigarettes.
   The Conversions.
   The Human Country: New and
   Collected Stories.
   The Journalist.

FOR A FULL LIST OF PUBLICATIONS, VISIT:
www.dalkeyarchive.com